The Witchcraft Murders

A Fernando Lopez Santa Fe Mystery

THE WITCHCRAFT MURDERS

A FERNANDO LOPEZ SANTA FE MYSTERY

James C. Wilson

SANTA FE

© 2024 by James C. Wilson
All Rights Reserved
No part of this book may be reproduced in any form or by any electronic or mechanical means including information storage and retrieval systems without permission in writing from the publisher, except by a reviewer who may quote brief passages in a review.

Sunstone books may be purchased for educational, business, or sales promotional use. For information please write: Special Markets Department, Sunstone Press, P.O. Box 2321, Santa Fe, New Mexico 87504-2321.
Printed on acid-free paper

LIBRARY OF CONGRESS CATALOGING IN PUBLICATION DATA
(ON FILE)

WWW.SUNSTONEPRESS.COM
SUNSTONE PRESS / POST OFFICE BOX 2321 / SANTA FE, NM 87504-2321 /USA
(505) 988-4418

Graves at my command have waked their sleepers,
ope'd and let 'em forth by my so potent art.
—Shakespeare, *The Tempest*, Act V, Scene 1

Night Meeting

Fidel Rodriguez sat at his keyboard editing. He'd missed deadline again this evening. His managing editor would be pissed. The other reporters had gone home for the night, but the copy desk still waited for his story. As the *Santa Fe Independent*'s lead investigative reporter, Fidel ended up with the difficult stories. That is, the dangerous stories. This latest concerned the body of a young woman found in Los Cerrillos who had yet to be identified. Her naked body was found yesterday morning lying in front of the Cerrillos Hills State Park, about twenty miles south of Santa Fe. What most puzzled him was that the body had been wrapped tightly in a clean white sheet, head to foot. So tightly it resembled a mummy.

Fidel had spent the better part of the day walking around the visitor center, looking for clues that would explain the mystery of the mummy woman, as the *Independent* referred to her in their headlines. He planned to return tomorrow morning, maybe hike into the hills to see what he could find there. He still hadn't made sense of what he'd been told by the Santa Fe County Sheriff's Office. He needed more time to investigate.

Fidel checked his notes, most of which came from Larry Romero, the information officer for the sheriff's office. According to Romero, mummy woman had no visible injuries when examined by Forensics at Christus Saint Vincent Hospital. The lab could find no apparent cause of death, although it did find semen from three different men in mummy woman's vagina. This afternoon the only news worth reporting was the body had been sent to the Medical Examiner in Albuquerque who would, hopefully, determine a cause of death.

So Fidel added the update and hit the key, sending his story to the copy desk for final editing. He switched off his computer and stood up in the small newsroom, stretching his cramped legs. He'd spent way too much time at the keyboard today, waiting to hear from the sheriff's office. He needed more exercise and less sitting down. He gathered together his belongings, including his coffee thermos and lunch box, and stuffed everything into his backpack. He looked around to see if he'd forgotten anything when his desk phone rang.

"Fidel Rodriguez," he answered.

After a brief silence at the other end, a muffled male voice said, "Yeah...I have some information about the dead body found in Cerrillos... thought you might be interested."

Fidel sat back down at his desk. "Yes, I am interested. To whom am I speaking?"

Another silence.

"I'm a neighbor in Cerrillos," the man said. I can't say any more over the phone. I need to tell you in person. Can you meet me at the Cerrillos Hills State Park tonight, say about eleven o'clock?"

Fidel hesitated, debating the wisdom of meeting a stranger in such a lonely spot in the dark of night. "Uh...okay, I can be there," Fidel said, finally.

"Eleven o'clock at the visitor center," the man repeated and clicked off.

Fidel worried he was making a big mistake. The tiny village of Cerrillos was desolate enough during the day. By eleven o'clock tonight it would be totally deserted. Anything could happen out there in the dark.

Still, this might be his big breakthrough. He might find out more about what happened to mummy woman. He had to take his chances. What to do in the meantime, that was the problem. He had more than two hours to kill. He called his wife Dorothy and, when she didn't answer, left a message on their home phone. He told her he would be working late on the dead-woman-in-Cerrillos investigation and not to wait up for him. Then he went to the restroom and splashed water on his face. He didn't like the image staring back at him from the mirror: a slight, middle-aged man with bags under his eyes and short, thinning hair. He'd taken off his paisley necktie hours ago but still wore his corduroy jacket, the same tan corduroy jacket he wore to work every day. No doubt about it, he looked old and rumpled. Not to mention tired.

Since he had time to spare, Fidel decided to get something to eat before heading to Cerrillos. He left the newsroom and walked down Marcy Street to the coffee shop at the corner and bought a sandwich and cup of coffee. He sat in a corner booth where someone had left a copy of the Albuquerque daily newspaper and ate his sandwich slowly, while reading the newspaper. After he finished he left the newspaper in the booth for another customer to read and walked down Washington Avenue to the Plaza. Not many people out tonight, just a couple of homeless men panhandling on San Francisco Street and a lone musician strumming his guitar in front of Starbucks.

Fidel sat on a bench in the Plaza planning his day tomorrow. Depending on what he found out tonight, he would get an early start and pursue whatever leads the mystery caller gave him. If nothing else, he would return to the Cerrillos Hills State Park and search the trails. If he left his house at seven a.m., he could be back at the newsroom by Noon. Then he could call Deputy Sheriff Romero to see if there were any new developments in their investigation. That would give him plenty of time to write his next follow-up story.

Fidel exited the Plaza when it was nearly time to leave for Cerrillos. He walked quickly back to the *Independent* on Marcy Street. Before leaving he checked his email one last time and then went out to the parking lot and climbed into his Chevy Impala. He followed the Paseo around to Cerrillos Road, which in turn took him to State Road 14 headed south. He didn't like driving on this highway, especially at night. Too remote, too spooky as he approached the infamous New Mexico State Penitentiary, set back from the road in a blaze of lights. Infamous because the worst prison riot in U.S. history had taken place there, resulting in the death of thirty-three inmates. The place still had bad, bad vibes.

Beyond the penitentiary the night seemed to close in upon him. Fidel saw no headlights in either direction. The highway ahead stretched out into dark, triangular hills. A fickle quarter moon hung in the sky, wrapped in a shroud of high, thin clouds. Past Turquoise Hill he began looking for the turnoff to Cerrillos. Moments later he spotted a scattering of lights off to his right. He braked and slowed the Impala to a crawl, straining to see in the shadows just beyond the beams of his headlights. Finally he saw the intersection and turned right onto the county road that became Main Street within the tiny, tumbledown village that dated from the glory days of coal and turquoise mining in the 1880s.

Proceeding slowly Fidel followed the posted signs to Cerrillos Hills State Park on the north side of town. He spotted the visitor center up ahead, a rectangular building with a covered porch and an adobe half-wall out front. He pulled into the drive and let his headlights splash over the dark, deserted building. Pausing a moment, he looked for another vehicle or someone lurking in the shadows of the visitor center. He saw no one, so he switched off his engine and waited, debating how long to wait before calling it quits and taking off. He checked his watch. Ten minutes past eleven and no sign of the person he was supposed to meet.

While Fidel considered his options, it occurred to him the informant might be waiting for him on the porch of the visitor center.

So he decided to check out this one last thing and then leave. He opened the car door and stepped out of his Impala into the cool night air. He walked carefully across the parking lot, unsure of his footing in the dark. Somewhere out in the rolling hills a coyote howled, breaking the deafening silence. As he approached the dark porch he began to feel uneasy, on edge. Did he lock his car? He couldn't remember.

Suddenly Fidel heard footsteps behind him. He froze for a moment and then turned quickly, but not quickly enough. Out of the corner of his eye he saw a black object coming out of the darkness. He heard his skull crack as the object struck the side of his head.

Then he fell, falling into darkness.

1

Private Investigator Fernando Lopez found himself in a good mood this morning, a rare occurrence. His private eye business had new life, thanks to Athena Doering's $25,000 check for persuading her abusive, philandering husband Sonny to sign a divorce agreement and get the hell out of her life. Fernando had made Sonny an offer he couldn't refuse, with a little timely help from his Smith & Wesson. With Athena's check Fernando had been able to pay all the bills he'd accrued over the past few months working *pro bono*. Now he had a fresh start.

Fernando drove down to his office on Canyon Road every morning, usually between nine and ten o'clock. His office was an old carriage house garage his friend and landlord Ruby Montez let him use rent-free. He'd added wood paneling, carpeting, and office furniture, including a mini-frig to keep his Modelo cold. Since retiring, he took his sweet time coming down in the morning and closed the office whenever it suited him. If he wasn't working on a case, he usually called it quits around four o'clock and headed either home to his adobe on Acequia Madre Street or down Canyon Road to the El Farol bar for drinks. The artists on Canyon Road gathered religiously at El Farol every afternoon for happy hour and to bitch about the tourists. None of them bitched louder than his landlord Ruby, a potter who owned the gallery next door and a pottery co-op down in the Railyard District.

Today Fernando had arrived at his office later than usual, a few minutes past eleven o'clock. He checked his answering machine and found only one message from an elderly woman on Agua Fria who needed help finding her missing cat. No thanks. He called her back and told her to check the animal shelter. That taken care of, he decided to go next door to Ruby's gallery and offer to take her to lunch at El Farol. Before leaving, he made sure his filing cabinet was locked. Then he grabbed his cell phone and changed his window sign from 'Open' to 'Closed.'

When Fernando opened the door to leave he was surprised to see a small woman walking down the gravel path to his office. Bent over and appearing distraught, the woman looked familiar. Then he recognized Dorothy Rodriguez, the wife of Fidel Rodriguez, one of his oldest friends in Santa Fe. Fidel was the most experienced reporter writing for the *Santa Fe Independent*.

Usually impeccably dressed and proper, Dorothy wore what looked like her pajamas, loose fitting baggy pants with a gray sweatshirt pulled over her disheveled gray hair. Fernando knew something was terribly wrong by the look on her thin, pinched face.

"Dorothy?" he greeted her as she approached. "What's wrong?"

She burst into tears and threw her arms around him, weeping onto his shoulder.

Suddenly Fernando knew in his heart what was wrong but didn't want to say it out loud for fear it would come true.

"Fidel's dead!" Dorothy wailed. She held onto him even tighter.

Fernando's spirits sank. He held her tight and stroked her hair. "I'm so sorry, Dorothy."

"Last night Fidel didn't come home," Dorothy said, trying to catch her breath. "A county sheriff found him this morning out in Cerrillos. He was lying in the parking lot of the Cerrillos Hills State Park Visitor Center."

"Come in, let's talk," Fernando said, noticing bystanders on the sidewalk staring at them. He helped her into his office.

Dorothy sat in the chair across from his desk. She took out a tissue from a small pack she carried and dabbed at her eyes.

"Can I get you some water?" Fernando asked. "I keep bottles of water in my mini-fridge."

Dorothy shook her head.

"What was Fidel doing at the Cerrillos Hills State Park?" Fernando asked.

"I don't know," she said. "He called me yesterday evening and left a message, said he was working on another follow-up to the story about the dead woman found at the visitor center. He must have gone out there to interview someone."

"So that's why he went there last night," Fernando mused.

"Yes, because he's been following developments in the story—that the dead woman had no visible injuries and the sheriff didn't know what killed her."

Fernando considered. He vaguely remembered the story. "The dead woman who was wrapped in a white sheet?"

Dorothy nodded. "They sent her body to the Medical Examiner in Albuquerque, hoping the lab could identify the cause of death."

"I remember it now," Fernando said.

She stared at him. "I'm hysterical one minute and then angry the next. I don't have any faith that the Santa Fe County Sheriff will find Fidel's killer. They think it might have been a robbery attempt gone bad, but nothing was taken from the car. And Fidel would never have driven down to Cerrillos in the middle of the night unless he was going to meet a source. Somebody had to set him up."

Fernando agreed. "Yeah, Fidel was always very cautious."

"So I've come to ask if you'd take the case, find out who killed him," Dorothy said. "I can pay you for—"

Fernando raised his hand. "Not necessary. Don't worry about it. Fidel was my friend. I'll do my best to find his killer."

Dorothy lowered her head. Tears ran down her cheek again. "I know it's not very Christian, but I want whoever did this dead. I want him to pay with his life, just like he took Fidel's life."

"No, I think that's a natural reaction. It's understandable."

Dorothy did not respond.

"In the meantime is there anything Estelle and I can do for you?" Fernando asked. "What can we do to help?"

Dorothy held her head in her hands and wept. "Maybe. I'm overwhelmed right now. I haven't even taken a shower today. I'll probably call Estelle later. Maybe she can help with the mortuary arrangements, all that stuff. I just can't deal with it right now."

"She'd be glad to help," Fernando said.

Dorothy dried her eyes. "Oh, before I forget, here's Fidel's reporter's notebook," she said, reaching for her back pocket. "This was in the hospital bag with his other belongings."

Fernando took the narrow, four-by-eight-inch notebook bound at the top and placed it on his desk. He opened it quickly and saw Fidel's handwriting. "Thanks, maybe this will give me some idea why he'd gone down to the visitor center."

She nodded. "I hope so. I didn't show it to the deputies. I guess I should have, but I just don't have much faith in them."

Fernando shook his head. "Yeah, you should have at least told them about the notebook. Let me look at it first."

With this, Dorothy got out of her chair and shuffled to the door. Fernando noticed she was wearing her bedroom slippers.

Dorothy stopped at the door and, without turning around, said, "Thanks, Fernando. Fidel always liked you."

"I liked him too, Dorothy," Fernando said. "Fidel and I go way back. Don't worry, I'll find who killed him. I promise you that."

She nodded and walked out the door.

2

As soon as Dorothy left, Fernando called Larry Romero, the chief information officer at the Santa Fe County Sheriff's Office. He'd known Larry for years but hadn't talked to him since retiring. "Hey, Larry, it's Fernando Lopez," he said, when Romero answered.

"Fernando! How you doing? Long time no see," Larry said. "What's up?"

"I'm good," Fernando said. "I'm calling about Fidel Rodriguez, the *Independent* reporter found dead in Cerrillos this morning? What do you know so far?"

"Not much, because I don't have the report yet," Larry said. "All I know is that he was found dead in the parking lot of the Cerrillos Hills State Park Visitor Center. Apparently he was hit in the back of the head with a blunt object. Crushed his skull."

"You think it was a robbery?" Fernando asked.

"Well, that was mentioned as a possibility, but I don't buy it," Larry said. "I'd like to know what the hell Rodriguez was doing down there in the middle of the night?"

"Exactly," Fernando said. "And what about the woman who was found dead in the same place a couple of days ago—the one who was wrapped in a sheet like a mummy? Are the two homicides connected?"

"Good question," Larry said. "We don't even know if mummy woman was a homicide. Hell, we haven't even identified her. She was naked as a jaybird in that sheet, without any clothes or identification," Larry said, chuckling.

"What's the latest on her?"

"Not much yet," Larry said. "Forensics couldn't determine the cause of death, so they sent her body down to the Medical Examiner in Albuquerque yesterday. We haven't heard back yet. You know how that goes, usually takes a while."

"Yeah, I know," Fernando said. "They don't do anything fast. So who's conducting the investigation?"

Larry paused. "That would be Williams. She's been assigned to both cases."

"Jodie?"

"Yep, both cases," Larry said. "I don't think she's happy about it, but we're short-handed big-time. Gets worse every year. Legislature doesn't give us enough money. Then they complain about the rising crime rates."

"I know...they never have," Fernando said. "Is Jodie there now? Can you connect me?"

"No, she hasn't returned yet," Larry said. "As far as I know she's still in Cerrillos."

"Thanks, Larry," Fernando said and hung up.

Fernando smiled. He knew he could count on Jodie for help. He'd worked closely with her as a Santa Fe Police Detective on the Three Hills Ranch case and more recently as a private investigator on the Pecos Holy Ghost case. He trusted Jodie, one of the best cops he'd seen in his thirty plus years of law enforcement.

Fernando decided to skip lunch and drive down to the Cerrillos Hills State Park. First, though, he flipped through the pages of Fidel's reporter's notebook. At first glance it looked like Fidel's notes contained only the same preliminary information that Larry Romero cited. Nothing new. Then he saw a note scribbled at the bottom of one page: "rolled towel like pillow under head of dead woman."

That gave him pause. Why put a pillow under a dead woman's head? Did her killer, or whoever dropped her at the visitor center, think she might wake up? Made no sense to Fernando.

Fernando decided to try to catch Jodie before she left Cerrillos, so he deposited Fidel's notebook in his desk and placed the 'Closed' sign in his office window. Then he locked the door and walked down the gravel path to the parking lot. He climbed into his Cherokee and drove down to the Paseo and around to Cerrillos Road, a tangle of fast food restaurants and cheap motels. Heavy traffic and too damn many stoplights slowed him down on Cerrillos Road. It took forever to reach the exit to State Road 14, the two-lane highway known as the back road to Albuquerque. About twenty miles south of Santa Fe was the town of Cerrillos, if you could call two hundred people living in a tumbledown relic of the 1880's mining wars a town. Fernando didn't. He called it a movie set, because that's what it looked like to him: an Old West movie set. He knew for a fact that several western movies had been filmed there.

If he remembered his history correctly, always a big if, the Cerrillos mining boom began around 1879 and skyrocketed when the

Atchison, Topeka and Santa Fe Railroad built a depot at Cerrillos Station. Before long some two thousand mines dotted the Galisteo River Valley around Cerrillos producing turquoise, gold, copper, silver, and whatever else of value they could plunder. The history of Cerrillos and Madrid, its neighboring town, bored Fernando to tears, always had. But those interested in looking at dead mines could get their kicks by wandering around the trails of the Cerrillos Hills State Park.

As soon as he turned right on the spur that became Main Street, Fernando realized he'd forgotten how to get to the park. He drove down Main Street past the rustic Black Bird Saloon until he noticed a sign directing him to the visitor center on his right. He spotted Jodie's Santa Fe County Sheriff's cruiser in the parking lot. Relieved, he pulled into the lot behind the black and white cruiser and climbed out of his Cherokee. Then he walked up to the visitor center looking for Jodie.

"Fernando, what are you doing here?" came from somewhere behind him. He spun around and saw Jodie coming down the nearest trail waving her arms. She wore her officer's uniform and a black hat pulled down low on her forehead, almost touching her reflecting sunglasses. A tall, muscular woman, Jodie had played on the University of New Mexico women's basketball team for three years. Since then she hadn't lost any of her conditioning.

Fernando waited for her in front of the visitor center. "Dorothy Rodriguez asked me to help find Fidel's killer. She said one of the deputies thought it was a burglary, but she was dubious."

Jodie shook her head. "Not me. Whoever killed mummy woman set him up. Fidel had been nosing around here looking for clues, writing updates for the *Independent*. Must have made the killer nervous."

Fernando looked around. "Where was his body found?"

Jodie pointed to the side of the visitor center. "Over there where you see the yellow tape. Forensics came this morning but didn't find much. Some footprints that may or may not be the killer's. Not much else. We impounded Fidel's car, but that won't be any help because the attack occurred outside the car. His skull was cracked open by a crow bar or maybe a tire iron. We didn't find anything like that at the scene. So there you have it. Not much to go on."

Fernando nodded.

"We've posted notices and gone up and down the streets asking if any of the residents saw strange vehicles here last night, or the other night when the killer dropped off mummy woman," Jodie continued. "So far, nothing."

Thinking, Fernando kicked at the dirt path that branched off into multiple trails. The trails snaked up into the dusty rolling hills of the park, pock-marked with sagebrush and piñon trees and an occasional gnarly juniper. "So is there anything new on mummy woman? Larry said her body had been sent to the Medical Examiner in Albuquerque."

"We haven't heard back yet," Jodie said.

"What do you make of it so far?" Fernando asked.

Jodie chuckled. "Bizarre! That's what I make of it. You should have seen the body of the dead woman when Forensics removed the sheet. Not only were there no bruises or visible injuries, the body was immaculately cleaned and oiled. I swear to God, it looked as though the woman had just come from a spa. What kind of killer gives his victim a beauty treatment before he kills her—or to the corpse after he kills her? And how did the woman die? What killed her? Forensics had no idea."

"Jesus," Fernando said. "And I saw in Fidel's reporter's notebook, which Dorothy gave me, that the first responders found a towel under the woman's head. Like a pillow."

"Exactly, what's that all about?" Jodie asked. "Forensics took the towel to look for fingerprints."

Fernando looked up at the trails and frowned. "What's your next move?"

Jodie shrugged. "What I'd like to do is go up to the Black Bird Saloon for a drink," she said, laughing.

Fernando checked his watch. "Aren't you on duty?"

"No, my shift ended an hour ago," Jodie said.

Fernando smiled. "Well, then, let me buy you a drink. I need to pay you back for saving my ass in Pecos this past summer."

"Yes you do," Jodie said. "Yes, you do."

3

Fernando followed Jodie around to the Black Bird Saloon, an Old West style building with what looked like hitching posts out front. The only thing missing were the horses. A tin roof on the porch and huge panel windows greeted them as they parked in front of the venerable saloon. The dark colors and the curtains covering the bottom halves of the windows gave the Black Bird a shrouded, secretive appearance. Walking into the saloon was like walking through a time warp back to the 1890s.

Inside they found a room filled with wooden tables and spindle back chairs. Across the way a mottled brown antique bar looked like someone had tried to refinish it but gave up after scraping off about half of the ancient varnish. Above the bar hung a painting of horses, joined by a collection of deer heads with antlers on the walls. One old geezer wearing overalls and a baseball cap sat at a table in one corner of the room chatting with a woman of indeterminate age who turned out to be the hostess and server.

"Sit wherever you like," the woman said, smiling. Dressed in black, she wore her red hair tied in back, bright red lipstick, and blue glasses. More Sarah Palin than Lucille Ball.

Jodie chose a table in the opposite corner of the room. Fernando joined her.

The woman followed them over to the table. "Howdy, my name's Lulu. What can I getcha? Menus?"

"No, thanks, we just want drinks," Jodie said.

"I'll have a Modelo Especial," Fernando said.

Jodie nodded. "I'll have the same. It's too early for wine."

While Lulu went to get their drinks, Jodie went to the restroom. Both of them returned at the same time. "Here you go, honey," Lulu said, placing two cold bottles of Modelo Especial on the table. "Either of you want a glass?"

"Yes, please," Jodie said.

When Lulu brought their glasses, Jodie stopped her and said, "We're here investigating the two bodies found over by the park visitor center. Have you heard anything over there the last few nights or seen anyone who looks suspicious? Anything at all unusual?"

"Well, let me tell you something," Lulu snapped. "No one in Cerrillos would do such a thing, kill those two people. I'll tell you right now it's all these outsiders coming in to hike in that damn state park or climb Devil's Throne. I hear some of them are even building houses out there in the desert. You know, squatting! I told them not to open that state park, that it would be an invitation to trouble. All these strangers coming here, this was bound to happen."

Jodie frowned. "But have you seen anyone in particular who looked suspicious?"

"Hah! Just about every stranger who comes in here looks suspicious to me, especially the young ones," Lulu said. "If you didn't have that uniform on, I'd think you two were suspicious."

"Fair enough," Fernando said, trying to ease tensions. "Here's my card, if you do hear or notice something that raises your eyebrow."

Lulu tucked the card in her pocket and walked away, rejoining the old geezer in overalls.

"Well, that went well," Fernando said.

Jodie laughed. "Yeah, certainly did."

They drank their beers in silence for a while. Finally Jodie asked, "So what do you make of this mummy woman, all wrapped up in a sheet and laid out on a pillow? You never said."

Fernando shrugged. "You said it earlier—bizarre. I don't understand why the killer would go to so much trouble with the corpse of his victim. Why wash it and wrap it in a sheet and then place its head on a pillow? Did the killer think the corpse would wake up?"

"Maybe the killer wasn't a killer," Jodie said. "Maybe the woman was a friend of his who died suddenly and unexpectedly during sex, for example. Maybe he just wanted to drop off the body at a place where she would be taken care of...like a government facility."

"Okay, but why wouldn't he leave her with identification so she could be officially buried?" Fernando asked. "And what about Fidel? How would you explain that? Different killer?"

Jodie sighed. "Beats me. I don't know what to make of it."

By the time they finished their beers, the autumn light was already fading from the big windows in front of the saloon. Fernando left a twenty dollar bill on the table and waved to Lulu, who waved back. "You come back, now," she said.

Fernando stopped on the porch and turned to Jodie. "Will you keep me in the loop? Pass along any new information about Fidel or mummy woman."

"Will do," Jodie said, climbing into her cruiser and driving off, back to State Road 14 to Santa Fe.

Fernando stood on the porch trying to decide what to do next. It was too late to hike the trails and probably not worth his time anyway, since Jodie had already done that. So he called it quits for the day and followed Jodie back to Santa Fe. From Cerrillos Road he took the Paseo around to Acequia Madre and turned into his driveway, spotting Estelle's Camry in their garage.

He parked behind the Camry and walked though their garden, under towering cottonwood trees already beginning to lose their leaves. When he opened the back door, he found Estelle in the kitchen placing a tray of enchiladas in the oven, leftovers from last night's meal at La Fonda. Fernando smiled when he saw how youthful she looked in jeans and a cotton sweater. Petite and athletic, Estelle hadn't lost her energy or her looks. Her black hair was only beginning to streak with gray, while his was all salt and no pepper. Unlike his deeply lined face, Estelle's was virtually free of wrinkles. No doubt about it, she had aged much better than he had.

"Dorothy called and told me about Fidel," Estelle said as he walked into the kitchen. "I cancelled work tonight so I could go over and sit with her. Some of our other friends are coming too."

"That's good...she was a mess when she came to my office this afternoon," Fernando said. He quickly set their kitchen table and then went to the refrigerator and grabbed a Modelo. "She wants me to find Fidel's killer."

Estelle turned and stared at him. "Well, you just better be careful. You're supposed to be retired now, remember?"

Fernando nodded and opened his Modelo. "Don't worry. I'll be careful."

Estelle shook her head, unconvinced.

4

Estelle was just leaving for work when Fernando awoke. She'd come home late last night after spending the evening with Dorothy. Estelle insisted on keeping busy these days. Unlike Fernando, who cut back once he retired, Estelle worked long hours for the Saint Francis Immigrant Outreach Program, a church-sponsored nonprofit that provided food and clothing and other services to Santa Fe's growing immigrant community. In fact, her workload kept increasing as more and more immigrants came through Santa Fe, a sanctuary city.

Fernando hated to admit it, but he and Estelle were no longer as close as they once were. Estelle had grown more religious over the years, working for the outreach program and attending mass almost every Sunday. He had grown in the opposite direction. After thirty years of police work he'd lost his faith. He believed in a material world, pure and simple. He still went to church with Estelle on Christmas Eve and Easter Sunday just to appease her, but that was as far as he was willing to go.

He splashed water on his face and dressed quickly, avoiding the mirror. He'd become superstitious about the mirror, believing every time he looked in the mirror he got older. If he stopped looking, he wouldn't age.

Dressed, Fernando went to the kitchen and poured himself a cup of cold coffee from the pot Estelle had left on the counter. He warmed it in the microwave and then made himself a ham and cheese omelet for breakfast. While eating he made a plan for the day. First he would go back to Cerrillos and explore the dirt roads branching out into the desert. Lulu at the Black Bird Saloon had mentioned all the outsiders building homes in the area around the Cerrillos Hills State Park and Devil's Throne, whatever that was. He'd never heard of Devil's Throne.

After that, he didn't know what the hell he would do. Go back to his office and wait for developments probably. Maybe call Forensics and hear what Teresa and Miguel had to say about mummy woman.

With that, Fernando strapped on his Smith & Wesson and made sure it was loaded. He wanted to be prepared, just in case. In case of what, he didn't know.

After locking their front door, he climbed into his Cherokee and drove down to the Paseo and around to Cerrillos Road, crowded at this hour by commuters coming to work in Santa Fe from outlying communities where they could still afford to live. The median price of a house in picture perfect Santa Fe had surpassed seven hundred thousand dollars, a lot of money for your average working stiff. Most of the people he knew were older and already owned homes. If they didn't, they would be out in the boondocks with everyone else. That was the dirty little secret here: only the wealthy could afford to live in Santa Fe today.

From Cerrillos Road he turned off on State Road 14 and headed south past the penitentiary. Bright sunshine illuminated the triangular hills ahead of him. He passed Turquoise Hill and the turnoff to County Road 45 and Picture Rock. He slowed down as he approached Wolf Road, an unimproved dirt road that seemed to meander aimlessly and then peter out in the distance. He bypassed Wolf Road and continued on down to the Cerrillos turnoff. This morning he didn't see Jodie's cruiser or any other vehicle in the parking lot of Cerrillos Hills State Park Visitor Center.

Not stopping, Fernando drove through Cerrillos on what became Waldo Canyon Road, another unimproved dirt road. His Cherokee kicked up a wall of dust as it negotiated the washboard road, driving through rolling hills of sagebrush and chamisa, with an occasional piñon tree to break up the monotony. Minutes later he saw a couple of cars parked off the road up ahead. When he saw the metal 'No Trespassing' sign he realized he was approaching Devil's Throne.

Fernando pulled off the road and parked next to the other cars, an old Subaru Outback and a new Toyota Rav4 with Texas license plates. He laughed as soon as he hopped out of his Cherokee and looked up at Devil's Throne, an enormous rock about the size of a two-story house with a sheer cliff facing the parking area. Two climbers wearing shorts and pointy climbing shoes clung like lizards to the cliff, inching up one toehold at a time. Fernando laughed again. Why come all the way from Texas to climb a fucking rock in the middle of nowhere? He didn't get it. He could see climbing Santa Fe Baldy, for example. He'd climbed it many times when young. But a rock?

One of the climbers heard him laugh and turned to look at him. Fernando waved. The climber didn't.

Still laughing, he climbed back in the Cherokee and studied the landscape. Several trails or unmarked roads branched out into the hills from Devil's Throne. Some of them looked like routes created by all terrain vehicles. ATVs did more damage to the high desert than any invasive species, plant or animal. Some of the trails seemed to crisscross haphazardly.

Why not? He gunned the Cherokee and bounced up the nearest trail, dodging the deepest ruts and largest rocks. Bucking up and down, he crested the first hill and saw a vast panorama of sagebrush mesas and rocky hills etched by dry arroyos spread out in front of him. He stopped the Cherokee and stared at the rough terrain. He immediately saw what Lulu meant when she complained about outsiders moving in and bringing the locals trouble. The hills were pockmarked with RVs and homemade yurts, even teepees. There were also a few actual houses, some adobe and others of frame or log construction. Just who lived in these structures was anyone's guess. Talk about off-grid. This was textbook.

Fernando killed the ignition and took his binoculars out of the glove compartment. He climbed out of the Cherokee and scanned the hills, examining each of the structures in turn, studying their yards and the vehicles parked next to them. What was he looking for? He didn't really know, but he looked at every one of them anyway. Looked until his eyes got tired.

Finally he gave up and climbed back in the Cherokee. Maybe mummy woman came from one of these homesteads, if you could call them homesteads. Maybe her killer even lived here, he had no way of knowing and presently no way of finding out.

Giving up, Fernando drove through Cerrillos to State Road 14 and headed north to Santa Fe. On the way back he considered his options, slim to none. He wondered. Maybe his longtime friend Ruby would have an idea about how to proceed. Ruby seemed to know everyone and everything going on in Santa Fe.

Thinking about Ruby made him smile. He and Ruby went back a long way, even before he met and married Estelle. Always prickly, Ruby wore her bad attitude with pride. To her, it was a badge of honor. Her in-your-face personality put off many people but had made her a force in Santa Fe politics for over two decades. A potter by trade, Ruby had risen through the ranks of *La Raza* to become the most progressive member of City Council ever. Back in the 1990s she fought tooth and nail against all the greedy developers who wanted to turn downtown Santa Fe into one big shopping mall. She led rallies, marches, protests, sit-ins, and if you believed the rumors, a fire-bombing or two.

She lost, of course. The developers and the Sotheby's crowd turned

Santa Fe into Disneyland Southwest. The tide of gentrification sweeping over Santa Fe during those years hollowed out the city. Gone were most of the people whose families had lived in Santa Fe for generations. Increasingly higher home values and property taxes priced out all who couldn't afford the million dollar homes. After two tumultuous terms on City Council lecturing, berating, cajoling, and threatening the other members, she said 'fuck it' and retired to the pottery co-op she owned and ran with a number of other potters, most of them women.

Still she refused to be silenced. She made it a point to attend most Council meetings and give the members a piece of her mind. Every one of them feared Ruby's tirades. Occasionally her anger would get the better of her language and she would be asked to leave. Once a few years back City Council banned her for a year, but her lawyer, Raoul Garcia, sued their asses and got her reinstated in her front row seat staring down the Council.

Over the years he and Ruby had always been friendly, probably because they felt the same way about gentrification and Santa Fe politics in general. That is, they usually ended up on the losing side. So it goes.

Back in Santa Fe, Fernando drove around the Paseo and up Canyon Road to his office. He turned into the parking lot and pulled up next to Ruby's Honda Accord. Ignoring his office, he went next door to Ruby's gallery, The Three Cities of Spain, named after a famous Canyon Road restaurant that closed years ago. He stepped up on her porch and opened the door. Inside, the gallery's walls and shelves were a riot of color: vibrant pastel and oil paintings hung on the walls, and colorful ceramics filled the shelves that Ruby had added to what had been her dead ex-husband Jimmy Mackey's painting studio. He found Ruby sitting in her office at a make-shift counter she used for lunches and coffee breaks.

"Fernando, come join me for a cup of coffee," Ruby said, waving him back. Ruby's shoulder length black hair might have a streak or two of gray, but she was still the striking woman he knew from his youth: black, bedroom eyes and an irreverent, ironic smile that radiated sexuality. A force of nature, Ruby was both gorgeous and intimidating.

He pulled up a chair and joined her at the counter while she poured him a cup of coffee from her coffee maker. She placed containers of milk and sugar on the counter next to his cup.

"Have you heard about Fidel?" Fernando asked, pouring sugar and milk into his coffee cup and stirring the murky mixture with a spoon.

Ruby made a face. "Yeah...I'm so sorry. I know you two were close friends."

"He was a good man," Fernando said. "Helped me out on more cases than I can remember. He was always willing to help."

"So what happened? Ruby asked. "I read his news stories about the mummy woman they found in Cerrillos. Then I heard he was murdered in Cerrillos. What's that all about?"

Fernando told her everything he knew about the mummy woman, including that she had no visible wounds and that her body was immaculately washed and oiled inside the winding sheet. "The sheriff's office thinks Fidel was murdered by whoever killed the mummy woman. To stop the investigation."

Ruby gave him the Evil Eye. "You say this woman's body was washed and oiled before the killer wrapped it in a sheet? That sounds like a human sacrifice, some really sick shit!"

Taken aback, Fernando said, "Human sacrifice. I never thought of that. Now I'm even more worried."

"Who was this woman, anyway?" Ruby asked.

"They don't know," Fernando said. "She was naked in the sheet. No personal belongings or identification."

Ruby shook her head. "I don't know, Fernando. You might want to sit this one out. You don't want to end up mummy man."

5

Fernando tossed and turned all night long. Toward morning he dreamed he'd been turned into a mummy and was struggling to get out of a sheet wrapped tightly around him. He woke up with a start yelling, "No...I'm alive, I'm alive!" Then he heard voices. Estelle was talking on the phone somewhere in the house. He fought his way out of the bedclothes twisted around his body and sat on the edge of the bed trying to clear his head. Some mornings the fog in his brain just wouldn't lift. Another sign he was getting old, as if he needed any more signs.

Stretching, he pulled on his jeans and hiking shoes and stumbled down the hall. He found Estelle sitting in his office talking on the phone. She turned to him and said, "I'm talking to Helen, we're making plans to sort the clothes we've collected for distribution tonight."

Fernando nodded and continued on into the kitchen, where he poured himself a cup of coffee from the pot on the counter. He plopped down in a kitchen chair and sipped the coffee slowly, waiting for the fog to lift. It didn't.

Finished talking on the phone, Estelle breezed into the kitchen dressed for work and full of energy. She took her lunch out of the refrigerator and headed for the door. Suddenly she stopped and turned to Fernando. "Oh, I forgot, your friend Manny called earlier. I tried to wake you, but you were sleeping like the dead." Then she walked out the door, gone.

Things were moving too fast for him this morning. Time to slow down.

Fernando sat at the kitchen table shaking his head. Where did Estelle get her energy? Not drinking alcohol probably helped. He made a mental note to cut down his consumption of Modelo. And what did Manny want this early in the morning? He checked the wall clock and read half past nine. Not that damn early. He'd overslept. Again.

Looking around the kitchen, he saw Estelle had left him some scrambled eggs and sausage on the stove, so he ate that for breakfast and helped himself to another cup of coffee. Feeling better, he decided to call Manny. Before he could, his cell phone rang.

"Wake up, Sleeping Beauty," Manny said, sounding pissed. Unusual for Manny, who usually played the role of jester. "All hell's breaking loose this morning, haven't you heard?"

"I haven't heard anything," Fernando said.

"Well, first of all, we've established the identity of mummy woman," Manny said. "Her name is Gloria Chavez, thirty-eight years old. We ran her fingerprints and found a match. She's a professional hooker, a prostitute. Turns out we've picked her up a couple of times for soliciting. She works the big downtown hotels—Eldorado, Drury Plaza, Saint Francis, La Fonda, and the Inn at Loretto."

"No kidding?" was all Fernando could think to say.

"No kidding," Manny repeated. "The question is: what was she doing out in Cerrillos?"

"Whoever killed her probably picked her up at one of the hotels," Fernando responded.

Manny chuckled. "Yeah, I guess, but the Cerrillos types don't strike me as the kind of people who go to hotels looking for hookers. Bunch of old hippies and counterculture types. Know what I mean?"

Fernando did but wasn't going to give Manny the pleasure of admitting as much. "So what else is new? If that was the 'first' bit of news, there must be more. Is that right?"

"There is," Manny said. "I saved the best for last. A second mummy was found this morning outside the visitor center at the Cerrillos Hills State Park. I kid you not."

Stunned, Fernando did not respond.

"Are you still there?" Manny asked.

"Yeah. Who found the body?" Fernando managed to ask.

"One of the groundskeepers found it when he came to work about seven o'clock," Manny said. "Jodie's on her way to Cerrillos now. She wanted me to call you and let you know."

"Okay, thanks Manny," Fernando said and clicked off. He knew instinctively what he had to do.

Without thinking, he put away his dishes and finished dressing. He grabbed his Smith & Wesson and headed out the door. Within minutes he was racing down State Road 14 toward Cerrillos. What little traffic he encountered on the two-lane highway was coming into town, not going out. At the Cerrillos spur he turned right and drove into Main Street. From a distance he saw red-headed Lulu opening the front door of the

Black Bird Saloon. Then the visitor center, where Jodie was just stepping out of her black and white cruiser. Fernando pulled in behind the cruiser and waved at Jodie.

Climbing out of the Cherokee, Fernando saw two men standing over another mummy lying on its back in the parking lot. Like the first mummy, this one had a rolled up towel under its head. One of the men wore a Carhartt jacket and a CAT baseball cap, the other slacks and a button down shirt. Must be the groundskeeper who found the body and a clerk from the visitor center, he figured.

Fernando followed Jodie, careful to let her lead the way.

"Stand back, please," Jodie said and motioned for the two men to move back, which they did.

"I found it when I came to work this morning," the man in the baseball cap said. He appeared to be in his late forties or early fifties, with gray stubble and a sad, sorrowful look on his face. "I called right away."

Jodie nodded, squatting to examine the body. It was obviously another woman because of the curves and the two mounds on its chest. Like the first body, it was wrapped tightly in strips from a white sheet, like a mummy.

Jodie stood and turned to the man wearing slacks and a button down shirt. "When did you arrive?"

"Just a few minutes ago," the man said, an older man with fine white hair parted neatly on the side. He looked nervous, fidgeting with his car keys. "I saw Pete over here, so I came to take a look. It's a terrible thing for the park. People are going to think this is a dangerous place and stay away. I don't understand why the bodies are wrapped up like that. What's happening here?"

Jodie sighed, irritated by the man's complaints. "Some sicko is killing these women and dumping their bodies here."

"But why here? And why are they wrapped in sheets like that?" the older man persisted.

Jodie shook her head.

Suddenly the man wearing a baseball cap jumped. "Wait! Did you see that?" he shouted and pointed to the mummy. "Her leg moved. I swear to God!"

Jodie stared at the mummy. Her legs twitched again, bending ever so slightly at the knees.

"Whoa!" the older man said, moving further away from the mummy.

"Don't panic," Jodie said. "Sometimes the body's muscles flex after death. It's not that unusual."

Suddenly the mummy's head moved side to side. The man wearing a baseball cap stepped back, joining the older man.

Now Jodie looked concerned. She turned to Fernando. "Do you have a pocket knife?"

Fernando handed her the fishing knife he always carried.

Jodie squatted over the mummy again. She found a place on the side of the mummy's head where one strip of the sheet was knotted. Opening the knife, she sliced through the knot and pulled the sheet away from the woman's face, a young woman with pale, milky skin and blond hair, matted as though with heavy gel and sticking to her scalp. The woman's eyelashes fluttered and her head turned slightly toward Jodie.

"Jesus Christ! Call an ambulance," Jodie said to Fernando.

"See—she's alive," the man wearing the baseball cap said. He and the older man moved closer to get a better look at the woman's face.

Jodie caressed the woman's arm. "Miss? Miss? Can you hear me?"

The woman's eyes opened just a sliver and then closed again immediately. She lay still, seemingly exhausted by the effort.

Fernando called for an ambulance, while the others gawked at the woman who seemed to have been magically resurrected. Like Lazarus.

Fernando and Jodie stared at each other.

"Maybe that explains the pillow," Jodie said.

"What do you mean?" Fernando asked.

"In case they wake up," Jodie said. "Maybe whoever did this thought there was a chance his victims weren't dead—that they would wake up."

The four of them waited in awkward silence for the ambulance to arrive. Minutes later they heard the siren screaming down State Road 14. A welcome sound.

Soon the ambulance pulled into the parking lot behind Fernando's Cherokee. Two medics jumped out of the ambulance and stopped dead in their tracks when they saw the mummy woman. "You gotta be kidding me," the older of the two medics said. "Is this a joke? Or some sort of emergency preparedness practice?"

Jodie stood up and confronted them. "No! This woman was believed dead. Hurry, she needs your help."

The medic nodded, getting down on his knees and starting to unwrap the strips of sheet. When he exposed the woman's neck, he felt for a pulse. "She's alive!" he shouted to the younger medic, who rushed over carrying a medical bag in one hand and a stethoscope in the other.

The woman seemed to fade in and out of consciousness as the medics worked on her. They managed to unwrap enough of the strips to free one arm and start an IV. It took them nearly fifteen minutes to stabilize the woman. Then they moved her onto a stretcher and carried her to the ambulance.

By this time the groundskeeper and desk clerk had gone off to their separate jobs, leaving Fernando and Jodie standing in the parking lot listening to the siren grow fainter as it sped toward Santa Fe.

Jodie turned to Fernando. "What do you think?"

"Like watching the dead awake," Fernando said. "That's what I think."

6

Fernando and Jodie followed the ambulance to Santa Fe in their separate vehicles. From State Road 14 they turned right on Saint Michael's Drive. A few stoplights later they approached Christus Saint Vincent Hospital on the left side of the road. They parked in the lot nearest the Emergency Room and walked through the double doors. Inside, they found the Emergency Room nearly empty, with only one young mother holding a coughing baby in her arms and either a drunk or a homeless person passed out in a chair at the back of the room.

Jodie sighed walking up to the front counter. "I hate this place," she said, surprising Fernando. He'd never heard her express any weakness or even hesitation. Maybe she was human after all.

"Why's that?" he asked. Foolishly.

"I hate the idea of being sick," Jodie replied. "It doesn't figure in my playbook."

"Can I help you?" the young woman at the front counter asked, interrupting their conversation. She was a plump young woman with glasses and braided hair who looked exhausted, as if she were nearing the end of a long shift.

"Yes, we're here with the ambulance that just arrived—with the woman wrapped in a sheet," Jodie said.

The young woman sighed and checked her screen. "Okay, they've already taken her back. She's being seen now."

"We'd like to go back," Jodie said.

"Are you family?" the woman asked. "We're calling her Jane Doe until we find out her name."

"No, I'm a Santa Fe county sheriff and this is my assistant," Jodie said, pointing to Fernando.

Frowning, the woman stared at them. "You'll have to wait until she's stabilized. Then you can probably see her, depending on her condition."

Jodie stood at the counter for a moment staring back at the woman. Then she turned abruptly and stomped off to the first row of seats. Fernando joined her.

"You see what I mean?" Jodie asked.

"Hah! I thought you were going to say something you'd regret," Fernando said.

Jodie glanced at him. "If I would have said what was on my mind, I wouldn't regret it."

They waited for over an hour before the young woman waved them over to the counter. "Okay, she's out of radiology and been admitted to room four thirteen. You can visit her now unless they're in the middle of a procedure."

"Thanks," Fernando said. Jodie stood back a ways frowning at the woman.

They took the elevator to the fourth floor and found room number 413 across from the nurse's station. No longer bound up like a mummy, the young blond woman seemed to be resting comfortably in bed, hooked to a panel of monitors that beeped, flashed, and zig-zagged across the screen. Out of the sheet wrapping she looked much smaller and younger, a thin wisp of a woman who looked to be in her twenties. Quite attractive.

One of the head nurses wearing a white uniform stood reading the young woman's chart when Fernando and Jodie entered the room. "She goes in and out of consciousness," the nurse explained. "At times she seems to be hallucinating. We're waiting on the results of her blood work. Maybe she's taken some drugs. We should know soon."

"You're calling her Jane Doe?" Fernando asked.

The nurse nodded, a middle-aged woman with black, curly hair. "Until we know her identity."

When the nurse left, Fernando and Jodie sat in chairs next to the bed. Jane Doe's breathing made a rasping sound. She started to mumble and move her head from side to side. Was she starting to wake?

Suddenly Jane Doe's eyes fluttered. Then her mouth opened and she tried to scream, making a raspy, guttural sound. "No! Leave me alone!" she gasped, starting to move her arms.

Jodie stood up. "Miss? Can you hear me?"

The young woman started shaking and jerking in the bed. Looked like she was having a seizure. "Leave me alone! Get away! He's a witch! Help!"

Lights flashed and monitors beeped as Jane Doe pawed at the

connecting wires and IVs. The nurse in the white uniform rushed into the room, followed by a young tech in a blue uniform. "Get the restraints," the nurse said to the tech.

The nurse then turned to Fernando and Jodie. "You'll have to leave now. Immediately."

"Okay," Fernando said, and followed Jodie out of the room. Jodie paused and listened a moment and then walked quickly off the ward.

Fernando caught up with her in the waiting room next to the elevator. He checked his watch. "It's been a long day. You want to get a beer?"

Jodie shook her head. "No, I'm going to stay here a while. I need to call Manny at the station to get a police watch for our Jane Doe. We don't want to give the killer a second chance."

"Well, keep me posted," Fernando said and took the elevator down to the ground floor. The Emergency Room was starting to fill up now. People were lined up at the front counter waiting to be served. The young woman at the front counter looked even more exhausted than before.

Outside, Fernando climbed into his Cherokee and drove off, heading east on Saint Michael's Drive. He turned left on Old Pecos Trail and drove downtown. The Paseo took him to Canyon Road. Approaching his office he saw Ruby and the Bryans talking in the parking lot. Paul and June Bryan owned Essentia next door to the west of his office and weren't generally all that sociable. Had there been another break-in on the street? They'd had several robberies already this year.

He parked next to Ruby's Honda Accord and jumped out of the Cherokee. "What's up?"

"We were just commiserating about the lack of business now that the tourist season is almost over," Ruby said. "Even though we hate the tourists, we love them too. If that makes any sense."

Fernando laughed. "Perfect sense."

"We're on our way to El Farol for happy hour," Ruby said. "You coming?"

That the Bryans were coming surprised Fernando. He hardly ever saw the Bryans at El Farol, especially during happy hour.

"Just one," June said, a tiny woman with blue hair who always wore a leotard and looked pre-pubescent. Today she had a see-through skirt on over the leotard and ballet slippers on her feet.

Paul nodded, looking as dapper as ever in chinos and a long-sleeve polo shirt, with hair slicked back with so much gel it looked shellacked. Right out of a Brooks Brothers catalogue.

"Sure, I'll tag along," Fernando said, following them.

They walked down Canyon Road to the remodeled El Farol, its tan stucco trimmed with dark brown wood looking spiffy in the late afternoon light. Fernando waited for the others to enter and then stepped up onto the porch and through the front door into the cozy restaurant. A few of the old timers on Canyon Road hunkered down at the bar nursing their beers. Down below in the restaurant all the tables remained empty at this early hour except one, where Blaine Rogers sat waving at them. The owner of Picasso and Co. Gallery, Blaine was a serious drinker and hell-raiser. He could drink everyone under the table except maybe Ruby, who usually held her own. Ruby and Blaine were both friends and arch-rivals at the same time. They fought constantly over Ruby's dead ex-husband Jimmy Mackey's paintings, which Blaine sold at his gallery when Jimmy was alive. Now that Ruby had inherited the paintings, she insisted on selling them at her gallery. Both of them were larger than life. And loud.

"Come on back, I saved us a table," Blaine shouted, a big man who always wore outlandish clothes. Today he wore his usual red Bermuda shorts, a white T-shirt and a khaki fishing vest.

Ruby looked around the empty room and laughed. "Hah! I'll bet that was difficult."

Blaine frowned and then smiled when he saw June behind Ruby. "Hey, June bug, I need one of your magic massages," Blaine blurted out. "You know the kind I'm talking about. Later tonight?"

June blushed, but her husband Paul ignored both Blaine and June.

Penny, one of the regular servers at El Farol, came over to take their orders. A young beauty with short dark hair, wearing a tie-dyed T-shirt, she said to Fernando and Ruby, "I know what you two want." Then she turned to the Bryans. "What can I get you guys?"

June looked at Paul. "I guess I'll have a gin and tonic."

"Me too," Paul said.

"So how long have you been here, Blaine?" Ruby asked. "You look half crocked already."

"No way. I'm just getting started," Blaine said.

Penny brought their drinks quickly, a frosted glass of Modelo for Fernando and a margarita for Ruby, and the two gin and tonics.

Blaine finished the margarita he was drinking and waved the glass at Penny, who nodded.

Blaine turned to Paul and June. "So what brings you two prudes over to sin city?"

"Oh, Jesus Christ, Blaine, we're here to talk business, if you don't mind," Ruby said.

Blaine waved his arm sarcastically. "Talk. Who's stopping you?"

Ruby turned to the Bryans. "So like I said, I'm going to have to find some other way to boost sales. Maybe sell cheap prints. I was even thinking of buying one of those expensive espresso machines and giving away coffee just to get people in the gallery. Something that would appeal to the everyday yahoos who walk up and down Canyon Road looking for souvenirs or whatever.'

"Might be worth a try," Paul admitted.

"I mean, like today, this jackass came into the gallery and asked if I had any paintings of unicorns," Ruby said. "I kid you not, fucking unicorns. He said he wanted it for his kid's room. I told him to go to the Disney store at the mall. I should have told him I sell fucking art, not trinkets or kid's posters."

June nodded. "Well, we're also thinking about expanding our stock."

"Yeah, we're thinking about adding herbs to our line of sex toys, unguents and medicinals," Paul said. "Since Ye Olde Herb Shoppe closed, there isn't a store in Santa Fe specializing in medicinal herbs. People come into Essentia all the time asking for herbal remedies for stress and anxiety, impotence, all kinds of stuff."

June laughed. "One guy came in asking for stimulants. I told him we sell erectile dysfunction herbs like Eucalyptus and Ylang Ylang and Chan, which is wild sage. He looked at me and asked if they would revive someone. I thought he meant sexually, but the more I think about it, I wonder."

"Revive? You mean like from the dead?" Ruby asked, but June did not respond.

"No, forget herbs! That's nickel and dime shit—why don't you sell weed now that it's legal in the state?" Blaine asked. "Weed would go real nice with those massages you give, June," Blaine said, winking at June.

"What, you don't have enough weed dispensaries to supply your habit?" Ruby shot back.

"Hah! There's never enough weed dispensaries," Blaine responded.

Laughing at the two of them, Fernando leaned back in his chair and listened to the banter, finally beginning to relax after a long, stressful day.

7

When Estelle left for work next morning, Fernando finished the breakfast dishes and then waited impatiently for Jodie to call. He felt too agitated to drive down to his office just yet. He wanted more information about Jane Doe, her condition and what she was saying this morning, if anything. He brooded about what Jane Doe had mumbled yesterday about a witch. 'He's a witch!' she'd said. Was she referring to the person who'd abducted her? A fucking witch?

After about an hour of brooding, Fernando found himself going to the dark place, a place he wanted to avoid after his short bout of clinical depression a few years back. He needed to get out, get away for a while, so he decided to drive to Christus Saint Vincent Hospital and check on Jane Doe himself. Why wait for Jodie to call?

He locked the house and drove the Cherokee to Christus Saint Vincent. By the time he pulled into the big parking lot on Saint Michael's Drive the morning had all but disappeared. His watch read eleven o'clock. He walked through the big doors and took the elevator up to the fourth floor. Stepping off the elevator, he found Jodie talking to another woman in the waiting room outside the ward. The two women were huddled in chairs near the rear window.

Jodie waved him over and said, "Fernando, this is Vicki Roybal, a social worker at the hospital. We're talking about Jane Doe."

"Fernando Lopez," he introduced himself and sat in a chair facing them.

"We've had some good news," Vicki explained. "The young woman is awake and talking this morning. Her name is April Lux, twenty-four years old. She comes from San Angelo in West Texas but is currently homeless. She says she's hitchhiking to Denver to stay with her sister. Two nights ago she stopped for a drink at the La Fonda bar and ended up going home with a man she met there. She doesn't know his name, but he's the one who abducted her. He drugged and raped her and then dropped her at the Cerrillos Hills Visitor Center. She doesn't know why he wrapped her in a sheet."

Fernando nodded. "Okay."

"Looks like she'll be released tomorrow," Jodie added. "So we need to find her a safe place to say."

"Which is why I've been on the phone this morning with the Esperanza Women's Shelter," Vicki said. "April can stay there while she recovers. When she's ready to travel to Denver they can buy her a bus ticket."

"Will she be safe at the shelter?" Fernando asked.

"Yes, Esperanza has a security guard," Vicki responded.

"Can we see her now?" Jodie asked.

"Of course, you can go right in. She's dressed and even walking around a bit."

With that, Vicki took the elevator down to her office on the first floor. Fernando and Jodie walked down the hall to room 413. As they approached a doctor wearing a white jacket stepped out of the room. He was writing in a notebook.

"Excuse me, doctor," Jodie said, showing him her credentials. "We understand the patient in room four-thirteen was drugged and raped."

"Yes, that's right," he said, a tall, white-haired man wearing glasses. He glanced at his notebook and then continued. "Except we're not sure of the drugs. We received the results of her blood-work this morning. We found a significant level of Troponin, which means her heart stopped beating at some point...and we found a trace of Wolfsbane, which can cause cardiac arrest...but there were also traces of Sanjeevani and Rose of Jericho, both of which work as stimulants, similar in effect to smelling salts, so to speak. So it's a bit confusing."

Jodie frowned. "So it's like whoever gave her the drugs killed her and then brought her back to life? Is that what you're saying?"

"Well...that's what it looks like," the doctor said. "Unless she was given all of the drugs at the same time, but I've never heard of a cocktail like that. Really, I don't know. Makes no sense to me."

Fernando and Jodie glanced at one another.

"The social worker said she might be discharged tomorrow," Fernando interjected. "Is that still a possibility?"

The doctor nodded. "I think so. The EKG we did this morning showed minimal damage to the heart, so yes, I think it's likely she'll be discharged tomorrow around noon. Okay? Now you'll have to excuse me. I need to finish my rounds." He closed his notebook and walked off down the hall.

Shaking her head, Jodie walked into room 413. Fernando followed.

"Hello, April, my name's Jodie, I'm a Santa Fe County deputy sheriff," Jodie said, showing her credentials. "My partner's name is Fernando, he's a private investigator helping me out. We're the ones who brought you to the hospital yesterday. I'm sure you don't remember."

April sat in her bed wearing a white sweatshirt and stretch pants the nurses must have found for her on the ward. She was a heavy-set young woman with bangs and a round, moon face. "What do y'all want?" she asked.

"We're investigating your kidnapping," Jodie said. "Can you tell us what happened? We understand you were drugged and raped by a man you met at the La Fonda bar. Is that right?"

April nodded but said nothing. Suspicious, as though worried they were there to arrest her.

"Did your assailant tell you his name?" Jodie asked.

"He said his name was Steve, but I think he was lying," April said. "I saw a letter addressed to him and it had some weird foreign sounding name on it. Like from one of those north countries."

'You mean a Nordic country?" Jodie asked.

"Yeah, maybe. A foreigner."

"What did he look like?" Jodie asked.

"Not much," April said, chuckling. "I only went home with him for a place to sleep that night. He's a scrawny old thing, all bones and long fingers. Creeped me out because he kept wanting to poke and touch me all over, when I just wanted him to do it and get it over with."

"What else can you tell us?"

"He's tall with short black hair and skin white as milk, that's what else," April said. "Plus, he told me he was a professor of anthropology at the state university. I didn't believe him, though. He was too creepy."

"The University of New Mexico in Albuquerque?" Jodie asked.

"I guess," April said.

"Okay, so where did he take you after you left La Fonda?" Jodie asked. "Can you tell us the location of where he attacked you?"

April shrugged. "We drove down some highway a ways and into this little town. I know because I saw the lights. Then he drove outta town on this dirt road and turned off his headlights so I wouldn't see where he was taking me. That's what I thought, anyway. He drove real slow in the dark until he came to his house, if you can call where he lived a house."

"What do you mean?" Jodie asked.

"Well, he had this little adobe house built against a hill among some old Indian ruins," April said. "That's where he took me first. He didn't say nothing, not one word. He just pushed me down on the bed and got rough with me. He tore off my clothes and turned me over on my stomach and raped me. Luckily it didn't last long, a few seconds maybe, and then he shot his wad. Afterwards he pulled up his pants and told me to get dressed and took me out to what he called a pit house that he'd remodeled. Said it was one the Ancestral Puebloans lived in before they built stone cities like the ones in Chaco Canyon. It was round with some kind of black roof on it and real dark inside, like a cave or something. I couldn't see much, just some stone benches and a fire pit. He kept a fire lit and some candles on the benches, that was all I could see. He tried to be nice to me, like he was trying to make up for what he done to me. He made me some tea and told me to drink it. I was so thirsty by then that I drank it right down."

"You think the tea was drugged?" Jodie interrupted April.

April nodded. "Must have been. While I drank the tea he started telling me this long story about a young woman who died but was brought back to life by a witch. I remember feeling tired, not being able to keep my eyes open. I must have fallen asleep during the story, because the next thing I remember was waking up in an ambulance all wrapped up in a sheet and being taken to the hospital."

Jodie glanced at Fernando, who shrugged.

So did he do anything else to you while you were sleeping—or drugged?" Jodie asked.

April shook her head. "You mean sex? I don't think so, but I don't know for sure because I was out cold. The one thing I do know is he wrapped me up in a sheet like I was a corpse or something."

Now Fernando stepped forward. "Do you think you would recognize this place if you saw it again? Do you think you could find it on that dirt road?"

April sighed. "I dunno. Everything was so dark. I'd probably recognize the pit house, but not how to get there. The road wasn't straight. Lots of turns and curves. Be real hard."

"Would you be willing to come with us and try to find it?" Fernando asked.

April paused and then said, "I guess."

"We could pick you up tomorrow when you're released and take you on a tour of the area, see if you recognize anything," Fernando said. "Then we could drop you off at the Esperanza Women's Shelter. The social worker told you they would help you at the shelter, right? After you get your strength back they'll even buy you a bus ticket to Denver."

April nodded. "Okay. Just tell them to get me some decent clothes.

I don't want to be seen like this." She opened her arms wide as if to show them her cheap white sweatshirt.

Fernando glanced at Jodie.

Jodie nodded. "I'll make sure," she said and walked out of the room.

Fernando followed Jodie to the elevator.

Jodie turned to Fernando. "A professor of anthropology? At UNM?"

Fernando laughed. "That's what the lady said."

8

Turning into his parking lot Fernando noticed a panel truck carrying ladders on its roof parked over near Essentia. While he parked, two men climbed out of the truck. One man unlatched a medium height ladder from the top of the truck, while the other opened the cargo door in back and brought out a bulky metal sign. Looked to be about three feet high and four feet long. It was a new sign for Essentia, Fernando realized when he saw the lettering: Essentia, Sex Aides and Medicinal Herbs. Just as Paul had mentioned the other day at El Farol, Essentia would now be selling medicinal herbs as well as sex aides for those who thought sex required lots of gear, like fishing or camping.

Fernando jumped out of his Cherokee and followed the two men around Essentia's adobe half-wall. Painted bright pink with dark red trim, the sprawling structure had stained glass windows that reflected the sunlight so that the building looked like it was glowing from the inside like an alien flying saucer, very New Age. A perfect match for Paul and June Bryan, who'd moved to Santa Fe from Sedona a few years back. Typical of people from Sedona, the Bryans were a New Age couple in every sense of the word, including having an open marriage. Especially June, who seemed to live on a different galactic plane than the rest of them. At Essentia they offered yoga, acupuncture, massage, sex therapy, and aural photography. Their AuraCam 6000 just happened to be the only aura camera in the Southwest—outside of Sedona, of course.

Nut cases, to Fernando's way of thinking. And now they were getting involved in medicinal herbs, which rubbed Fernando the wrong way. In Santa Fe and northern New Mexico Hispanics had a long history of *curanderismo*, folk or traditional healing that addressed mind, body, and spirit. *Curanderismo* was taken seriously here; it wasn't for ignorant newcomers to trifle with. You didn't dabble in *curanderismo*. To become a curandero you had to live it. There were different kinds of *curanderos*, including yerberos, who worked primarily with herbs. That would be the kind of healing the Bryans would pretend to practice. God help them if they tried to sell themselves as *Hueseros, Parteras, Oracionistas,* or *Brujas.* Fernando didn't believe they were that brazen. At least he hoped not.

Fernando watched while the two workers set up the ladder to remove the old Essentia sign on the front of the building. While he watched, the door opened and June appeared, blue hair and skimpy leotards barely covering her prepubescent body. "Come on in, let me show you our new arrangement," June said.

Fernando followed June into the spacious front room splashed with color from the stained glass windows. The smell of incense gagged him. Through the smoky haze Fernando saw Paul standing at the counter. Behind him towered a wall of sexual toys—everything from masks, whips, dildos and inserts of one kind or another. Shelves on one side of the room offered oils, lubricants, and unguents to juice the body and stimulate the libido. Shelves on the other side of the room remained empty.

Paul pointed at the empty shelves and said, "That, my friend, is where we'll stock our medicinal herbs," he said, wearing his usual khakis and polo shirt, with hair slicked back with gel.

"Yeah, we're working with a well-known *curandero* from Galisteo," June said, not about to be left out of the conversation. "He's gonna supply the herbs and teach us how to prescribe them—which and how much. Come on back and meet him, he's in my yoga room."

June waved Fernando back. He followed her behind the counter and down the hallway to the yoga room, where an assortment of mats lay on the floor. Toward the back of the room a massage table stood beside a bookcase stacked with oils and creams of one kind or another. There, sitting in a rocking chair and holding a cane in one hand, slumped a shriveled old man who looked a hundred years old. As tiny as June, his face resembled a saguaro cactus, with wrinkles in his wrinkles. He wore dirty jeans and a black wool vest with Native American designs over a blue work shirt. On top of his head sat a greasy brown Stetson hat with a beaded band.

"Fernando, this is Gabe Rivera, the *curandero* I mentioned," June said. "Mr. Rivera, this is Fernando Lopez, our next door neighbor. He's a private investigator."

Gabe nodded.

"Howdy," Fernando said, wondering if the old man could actually stand up. He looked like a skeleton dressed in clothes. He looked vaguely familiar.

"Gabe works with his son Tomas in Galisteo," Paul said, smiling.

"Tomas is delivering the herbs we ordered this afternoon."

Fernando turned to Paul. "Yeah? What did you order?"

"Just the basics to start with," Paul said. "We ordered Alhucema or lavender for colic, wild sage for virility, Comfré for ulcers and kidney trouble, Guaco for anemia, Añhil del Muerto for liver problems, Moradilla for anxiety, and Yerba Buena for hangovers."

Paul turned to June. "What else did we order?"

"Don't forget Manzanilla," June said. "You can use chamomile for just about anything."

Paul nodded. "Yeah, and more will follow depending on the needs of our customers."

"Hmmm," Fernando said, skeptically. "Do you guys even know what the hell you're doing?"

Paul's face turned red. "Well, we're getting advice from Gabe." He motioned toward the old man in the rocking chair.

Fernando walked across the room to Gabe, who watched him approach with milky gray eyes. The old man looked like a stuffed dummy. His wrists were as thin as pencils.

"Do I know you?" Fernando asked. "I'm a former Santa Fe police detective. I had a case in Galisteo a few years ago. Man shot the neighbor's dog. Neighbor shot the man's cow. Then both of them started shooting at each other."

"That was a good dog," Gabe croaked, barely audible. "I shoulda killed the sonofabitch instead of his cow."

Fernando chuckled. "No, then you would have ended up in jail instead of just paying for his cow."

Gabe frowned. "So what do you want?"

Fernando ignored the question. "How long have you been a *curandero*?"

"Since my momma taught me," Gabe shot back.

"Yeah? What kind of *curanderismo* do you practice?" Fernando asked. "You just peddle herbs, or do you make house calls?"

"Not any more," Gabe said. "I'm too damn old. I just sell the herbs and tell my people what to do with them."

"Do you by any chance sell Wolfsbane?" Fernando asked, remembering that Wolfsbane was one of the drugs found in April's blood work.

Gabe's eyes opened wide. He stared at Fernando, suspicious. "Why are you interested in Wolfsbane? Tryin' to poison someone?"

Fernando shook his head. "No, but I know someone who was poisoned with Wolfsbane. Thought you might be the supplier."

"Hell no, you're outta luck," Gabe said. "Some low-life broke into my workshop last week and stole my whole supply of Wolfsbane and some other herbs. I ain't even gone through everything yet to see what's missin'."

"No kidding," Fernando said.

"You callin' me a liar, mister?" Gabe shot back.

Fernando held up his hands. "Calm down, old timer. I'm not calling you anything. I'm only interested in who broke into your workshop. Do you have a card with your address in Galisteo? Maybe I can help you find whoever robbed you."

Gabe stared at Fernando for a moment and then nodded. He reached behind him and pulled out an old leather wallet held together by rubber bands. He undid the rubber bands, opened the wallet, and searched through the items in the wallet. Finding an old yellowed business card, he pulled it out of the wallet and handed it to Fernando.

"You find him and I'll shoot the sonofabitch," Gabe said.

Fernando chuckled. "No, don't do that. If you shoot him, you'll just end up in jail. Let me take care of him."

"We'll see," Gabe said, putting the rubber bands around his wallet and stuffing it in his back pocket.

"I'll be out to see you soon. Don't shoot anyone in the meantime," Fernando said, still smiling.

"We'll see," Gabe said.

9

Jodie arrived late. This morning they planned to pick-up April at Christus Saint Vincent Hospital and deliver her to the Esperanza Women's Shelter. First, though, they wanted to take her back to Cerrillos. Revisiting the area just might jog her memory and help them find her abductor. Or so they hoped, having little else to go on. Gloria Chavez, aka mummy woman number one, wasn't talking.

When Jodie's cruiser pulled into his parking lot, Fernando stood waiting outside the office. "Sorry I'm late," she said as Fernando climbed into the cruiser. "Another shooting out in Nambe. Teenagers this time."

Fernando shook his head. "Can't they find anything else to do besides shooting each other?"

Jodie laughed. "Apparently not. And sadly, they all have access to guns. Lots of guns."

She drove fast around to Cerrillos Road and Saint Michael's Drive. By the time they arrived at Christus Saint Vincent it was half past Noon. They took the elevator up to the fourth floor and walked down the hall to room 413. They were surprised to find the room empty, with hospital staff cleaning the surfaces and changing the bed coverings. April had flown the coop. Not good.

Fernando made a beeline to the nurse's station. "Where's April Lux? We made arrangements to take her to the Esperanza Women's Shelter this morning."

The nurse at the station frowned. "She left about fifteen minutes ago. Said you were downstairs waiting for her."

"I heard," Jodie said, coming up behind Fernando. "Let's go. She's probably walking to Interstate Twenty-five, planning to hitchhike to Denver. We can still catch her if we hurry. We need her testimony."

They took the elevator down to the ground floor and ran outside to Jodie's cruiser. She gunned the big engine and took off fast on Saint Michael's Drive. Halfway to the interstate they spotted April walking on the right side of the road just before the Zia Road intersection.

Fernando pointed to the lone figure ambling down the road. In no particular hurry, she looked as though she were out on a morning walk or a leisurely stroll during her lunch hour.

"We got her!" Jodie said. She swerved, pulling over on the shoulder in front of April, who jumped to the side, frightened by the speeding cruiser.

April wore clothes provided by the hospital social worker: slacks, a long-sleeve T-shirt and a denim jacket. She carried a small hospital bag in one hand and nothing else.

Jodie climbed out of the cruiser and confronted April. "Where do you think you're going? We were supposed to pick you up, remember? Take you to the Esperanza Women's Shelter."

"Yeah, I decided to continue on to Denver instead of going to the women's shelter," April said, nonchalantly. "I can hitch a ride on the interstate. No problem. I'm good at hitchhiking. Been doing it for years."

"No, no, you're coming with us," Jodie insisted. "We need your testimony. You need to stay at the shelter at least until we can get your statement."

April shook her head. "Nah, I told you everything I remember. I'll just be on my way. I won't take up any more of your time."

Fernando glanced at Jodie, who was furious. She was so angry she could barely speak.

"Listen, you...." Jodie began, but stopped herself before saying something she would regret. She took a long, deep breath and then stepped up in April's face. "If you won't come with us willingly, I'll arrest you right here and take you in physically. Do I make myself clear?"

Fernando smiled. Jodie, a former athlete, was a good six inches taller than April and incredibly muscular. Fight or flight, either way April would have no chance against Jodie.

April stared at Jodie. "Well, don't you at least have to read me my rights?"

"Sure, if you want me to take you in and book you," Jodie said, opening the right rear door of the cruiser.

April said something under her breath that sounded to Fernando like, "fucking bitch!" Then she walked to the cruiser and climbed in the back seat.

Jodie slammed the door closed on April and then motioned to Fernando to get in the cruiser. All aboard, Jodie continued on down Saint Michael's Drive to the Interstate 25 on-ramp and headed south.

"Wait...where are we going?" April asked.

"On a quick tour of the Cerrillos area," Jodie said. "You never know, seeing it again might help you remember where you were taken. After that we'll drop you off at Esperanza."

April did not respond.

Outside of Santa Fe Jodie turned onto State Road 14 heading south. Minutes later they approached Cerrillos. The little village glistened, looking almost cheerful in the mid-day sun. They drove past the Black Bird Saloon, where several cars were parked out front. The lunch crowd. Then past the Cerrillos Hills State Park Visitor Center and onto the dirt roads branching out every which way through the sagebrush hills and flat-top mesas.

Jodie slowed to a crawl approaching Devil's Throne. The sight of the giant rock with its sheer cliff seemed to agitate April. She began rocking back and forth in the car seat and then banging her head softly on the rear window. Finally she started to moan, a low-pitched moan that sounded like a wounded animal.

"Are you okay?" Fernando asked.

"Suck it up," Jodie said, her typical response.

"I'm having flashbacks, bad memories," April said. "This is one of the places he took me. I don't know where else we went. It was dark—I couldn't see anything. Please! Take me back!"

Jodie stopped the cruiser, ignoring April's request. "Okay, but first look around at the roads here. Do any of them look familiar? You must have seen something on your way to his place."

"I didn't," April protested. "It was pitch black outside and I was scared to death. I don't remember anything."

Jodie sighed.

"I think she's telling the truth," Fernando said. "I think she would help us if she could."

"All right, whatever you say," Jodie said, not happy with either April or Fernando. She started the engine and shot off in a cloud of dust, swerving back on the dirt road to Cerrillos. None of them said a word on the trip back to Santa Fe, not a single word.

Jodie didn't slow down until she turned onto Cerrillos Road. On Cerrillos the stop-and-go traffic and stoplights forced her to slow down to the speed limit. She turned left on Siler Road and left again on Agua Fria and moments later pulled into the parking lot of the Esperanza Women's Shelter, a two-story facility located behind a chest-high adobe fence that enclosed a mostly barren yard with a few patches of brown Bermuda grass and wilting flower beds. Like most such facilities, Esperanza looked woefully underfunded.

Fernando and Jodie climbed out of the cruiser, but April didn't budge. Sighing, Jodie came around the passenger side of the car and threw open its back door. "Listen, you've been through some serious trauma. You can use your time here to recover. When you get your strength back, they'll give you a bus ticket to Denver, just like your social worker promised. As soon as we get your statement, you'll be free to go. Do you understand?"

When April didn't immediately respond, Fernando feared Jodie was about to drag her out of the cruiser. But April was smart enough to realize that Jodie meant business. Without speaking, the young woman climbed out of the back seat with her hospital bag and gave Jodie a mock salute. The three of them walked up the sidewalk to the front entrance, Jodie leading the way with April in the middle and Fernando bringing up the rear, just in case she tried to run.

An intake nurse greeted them as soon as they entered. The nurse, a young woman April's age wearing street clothes, took April back to the admitting room, while Jodie went into the office to complete the required paper work. Fernando waited awkwardly on a bench in the lobby feeling not only out of place but downright unwanted. More than one woman resident in the large common room in the back of the building gave him the Evil Eye. It became clear to him that men were not terribly popular at Esperanza Women's Shelter.

Jodie returned a few minutes later and motioned for Fernando to follow. They walked outside and climbed into the cruiser, where they sat in silence for a few awkward moments.

"Sorry," she said finally. "I don't have much patience for young women who behave stupidly."

Fernando shrugged. "You're not alone. Young people in general, women or men."

Jodie smiled. "Jesus, we sound like a couple of old geezers."

"Yes, we do," Fernando said. "Yes, we do."

Finally Jodie started the cruiser and said, "I'll try to get someone over here this afternoon to get April's statement before she takes off again, which I'm sure she will since she seems bound and determined to screw up her life. Sometimes you just can't help them."

"I don't imagine her statement will be any different from what she's told us already," Fernando replied. "If she does know more, she sure isn't eager to share it with us."

"So what now?" Jodie asked. "Where do we go from here?"

"I do have one new lead that I haven't mentioned," Fernando said. He told her about meeting Gabe Rivera, the *curandero* providing medicinal herbs to Essentia. "Gabe said his workshop in Galisteo was burglarized last week and his supply of Wolfsbane was taken, along with some other herbs. Wolfsbane's the same poisonous drug the hospital found in April's blood work."

Jodie frowned. "So what are you suggesting? That the person who stole Wolfsbane from Gabe Rivera is the same person who killed Fidel and mummy woman... and the same person who tried to kill April?"

"That's what I intend to find out," Fernando said.

10

The afternoon was fast disappearing by the time Jodie dropped off Fernando at his office. Three o'clock didn't give him much time to drive out to Galisteo and back. Should he wait until tomorrow when he would have more time? That was the question. He found a message on his answering machine as he sat down at his desk. He cringed when he saw the message was from Dorothy Rodriguez, no doubt wanting an update on his investigation into Fidel's murder. Unfortunately, he had no news, nothing to report. He felt guilty for his lack of results, but what could he do? The case had proved more difficult than he imagined.

Fernando pushed the 'play' button and listened to Dorothy's message: "Hi Fernando, it's Dorothy...I wanted to know what you've found out so far about Fidel's murder...I haven't heard from you, so I don't know what to think...and I wanted to tell you that we've decided not have a public funeral for Fidel...our sons are coming home tomorrow and we'll have a private memorial at our house with Fidel's ashes...he wanted to be cremated and his ashes scattered on top of Santa Fe Baldy...he loved to hike up to the top of that mountain...it was his favorite spot in the whole world, I think...I'm too old to hike up there, so I'm sending our sons... anyway, if you want to stop by, we'll be starting around seven o'clock... okay...bye."

Many years ago Fernando enjoyed hiking to the top of Santa Fe Baldy with Fidel and a couple of other friends. Back then, before Flavia and Adela were born, he had more time for hiking and fishing. Now, like Dorothy, he was probably too damn old to hike to the top of Santa Fe Baldy even if he wanted to, which he didn't. As a young man he had lots of energy to burn; now he wanted to conserve what energy he had left.

Having nothing new to report, he decided to return Dorothy's call later, maybe tomorrow morning. The need for something to tell Dorothy made the decision for him: he would drive out to Galisteo after all. At the moment he had only a couple of hours of daylight left to pay Gabe Rivera a visit, so he quickly locked up his office and climbed into his Cherokee. Back on the road he took Old Santa Fe Trail out of town until it became the Old Las Vegas Highway. At the intersection of Highway 285 he turned south to State Road 41, which took him to the village of Galisteo.

About the same size as Cerrillos, Galisteo resembled a collection of tumbledown adobe houses scattered by a giant hand around Nuestra Señora de las Remedias Church. To the south lay the so-called Galisteo Creek, a dry gulch that snaked its way through the desert sand. To the north the Galisteo Basin swallowed myriad ruins of thousand-year-old Ancestral Puebloan communities, most of them unexcavated. It was a severe, no frills landscape with few restaurants or other commercial amenities, but home to dozens of artists who prized the remote setting. Hotter than blazes in the summer, cold and stark in the winter.

As Fernando approached the village, the late afternoon sun irradiated the light brown adobes, turning their stucco a pale red color. Fernando turned left on the town's main drag and drove past the church. Following Gabe's directions, he turned right on La Vega and then took a dogleg left that ran straight into the Galisteo Basin, a seemingly endless expanse of saltbush, prickly pear cactus, and dried brown tumbleweed. He gunned the Cherokee and swerved onto the unpaved road, his tires slipping and sliding in the loose sand. Soon Gabe's roadside shop came into view on the right. A gray, unpainted wooden building, it looked like an old time general store out of the late 19th or early 20th century. Maybe it was, for all he knew.

Leaving the Cherokee on the shoulder of the road, Fernando walked through a patch of weeds to a well-worn path that took him to the wooden porch out front of the shop. The floorboards creaked loudly as he climbed the steps and walked across the porch to a tattered screen door. He noticed the screen had been kicked out at the bottom of the wooden frame as he opened the door and stepped inside.

"Hello?" Fernando asked, not seeing anyone in the room. Just a long wooden counter and shelves stocked with gallon jars of herbs. Each jar had a homemade label made by magic marker attached to the glass.

Suddenly Gabe stood up behind the counter, surprising Fernando. Without his Stetson, the old man's shriveled head looked like it was covered in bird feathers. Matted down bird feathers.

"Didn't see you back there," Fernando said, laughing.

"I heard you come in," Gabe said, standing unsteadily with the aid of his cane. He looked as though he were on the verge of collapsing at any moment, a pile of rags and bones. Yet he stood staring at Fernando, not particularly friendly and not particularly unfriendly.

"I thought I might take a look around, see what I can find," Fernando said. "How did the thief break in?"

Gabe shook his head. "Nothin's broken, so the only thing I can figure is he came in through the dog door. I used to have me a German Shepherd, a big one. Take a look." He pointed his cane at the back corner of the one-room structure.

Fernando walked over to take a look. The swinging dog door measured a good eighteen inches wide and maybe twenty or twenty-four inches high, large enough for a small to middle-sized man to crawl through fairly easily. Or a "scrawny" man, as April described her abductor.

"So what happened to your dog?" Fernando asked, trying to be friendly.

"He took sick. I had to put him down," Gabe said, staring at Fernando.

Fernando moved from the dog door to the shelves behind the counter, reading the labels on the jars as went. He didn't recognize the names of most of the herbs. One he did recognize. The jar labeled 'Cannabis' remained untouched. That, in itself, was unusual. If available, weed or other such drugs were usually the first things taken in a burglary. Even though legal in New Mexico, marijuana sold for a pretty penny. Easy to resell for a big profit.

"So what all was taken?" Fernando asked.

Gabe pointed his cane at one of two empty spaces on the shelves. "Well, I told you about the Wolfsbane back in town. He also took my jar of Rose of Jericho and a couple small bottles of Sanjeevani."

"But he didn't take the weed," Fernando said. "Interesting."

"Damn right, he could resell that and make some money," Gabe said. "Don't make no sense to me. You for damned sure can't sell Wolfsbane or Sanjeevani on the street."

Fernando laughed. "No you can't."

Gabe spit on the wooden floor. "I'm gonna have to buy me another big dog to keep in here. That way if I hear the dog bark, I can come out here and shoot the sonsabitches, whoever they are."

Fernando shook his head. "I don't know, Gabe. Better to keep your distance and report it to the sheriff. Let them handle it."

"Hah!" Gabe said. "The sheriff don't come out here. They don't give a damn about us. Only the city folk."

"Suit yourself," Fernando said. He wasn't about to argue with the man.

With that, Fernando stepped outside and walked around the ramshackle shed to the dog door in back. He found footprints, lots of them, but no other signs of an intruder. After he finished checking the area, he made his way back to his Cherokee. He sat in the Cherokee for a few minutes surveying the landscape. Come nightfall it would be easy for someone to park on the road or even on the open mesa and then creep up to the shop undetected. Too easy.

Fernando started the Cherokee and made a U-turn, heading for the highway back to Santa Fe, his mood as dark as the western sky.

11

Fernando spent the morning in his study researching Wolfsbane. What he discovered troubled him. The plant was indeed poisonous, especially the roots. If ingested, its toxins paralyzed the nervous system and slowed the heart rate, potentially causing the heart to stop altogether. In history and mythology Wolfsbane was associated with werewolves, vampires, and witches. During the Middle Ages witches were said to use the drug in spells and deadly potions. Some people believed Wolfsbane had the power to repel werewolves. Others believed that contact with Wolfsbane under a full moon could cause one to become a shape-shifter.

On the other hand, he found that Rose of Jericho was known as the resurrection plant. It had the ability to die and then be reborn. Some argued that when ingested as a powder or a tea, Rose of Jericho could bring the dead and dying back to life. The same for Sanjeevani, a mysterious and magical plant from India. Ancient Hindu scriptures describe Sanjeevani as a magical herb with supernatural powers that could cure disease and revive the dead.

When finished, Fernando found himself asking the same question: why would the abductor give his captives both a drug that would kill them and a drug that would revive them? Was it a strange cocktail that produced unknown symptoms, as the doctor at Christus Saint Vincent Hospital mentioned? Maybe a hallucinogenic? Or a mind-numbing drug like fentanyl?

Finally he called it quits and decided to eat a quick lunch before going to his office. He ate a turkey sandwich with potato chips and then locked the house. Taking his time, he cruised to the Paseo and around to Canyon Road, still thinking about the plants he'd researched. As usual he pulled into his lot and parked next to Ruby's Honda Accord. He'd just stepped out of the Cherokee when his cell phone rang. He fumbled for the phone in his shirt pocket.

"Fernando, I have something you need to hear," Jodie said. "I'm on my way to your office. Be there in ten minutes, okay?"

Jodie clicked off quickly before he could answer. How did she know he would be at his office? Sometimes she seemed to have extraordinary powers, both physical and psychic.

Shaking his head, Fernando walked down the gravel path to his office and unlocked the door. He put the 'Open' sign in his window, as if it really mattered. Anyone who turned up at his office either walked in or banged on the door, no matter what the sign said. Inside, he checked his messages and found one from Sargent Antonio Blake, his closest friend on the Santa Fe Police Department, asking if he were planning to attend Fidel's remembrance tonight.

Was he planning to attend? He hadn't made up his mind. He still felt some embarrassment that he hadn't made much progress in finding out who killed Fidel. Plus, the celebration would be a family thing, he reasoned. He was trying to talk himself out of going.

Just then he heard Jodie pull into the parking lot. He heard her footsteps on the gravel path, walking fast, as always. Then the door opened and in walked Jodie. She seemed to be in a good mood, something he hadn't seen in a while.

"Wait until you hear this," Jodie said. "We managed to get April's statement this morning. I recorded it on my cell phone too. Listen to this."

She sat in the chair facing him and placed her phone on the desk. She opened the iRecord app and clicked the play arrow.

Fernando sat back in his chair and listened.

"...like I was saying, after sex he took me down a stairway to his pit house...a round hole in the ground, kind of like a cellar, which he said was an old Indian ruin. We were both thirsty, so he brought out a bottle of wine first and we finished that. Then he poured us glasses of water... except mine tasted funny, so I sipped it slowly. The more I drank the better I felt, so I drank the whole glass. Meanwhile he started telling me about his work in anthropology, said he was an anthropology professor. He said he believed the old stories about witches and healers were real, not mythology...and that he was conducting experiments to prove they were real...that they really happened in a way only witchcraft could explain.

"By this time I was feeling drowsy. Real tired. I had a hard time keeping my eyes open. I thought he'd given me some of that date drug, whatever it's called, so he could have sex with me again...but instead he started on this long story about two brothers and their sister who died. He said they lived in a little adobe house by this big cliff and one day a rock fell on the sister's head killing her. The brothers went crazy with grief...

they wanted to bring her back to life, but didn't know how. So they buried her near the big cliff and kept watch on her grave day and night, so no one could steal her body, because that's what they did back then, the witches, they stole bodies to use for their own selfish purposes.

"But by and by a witch smelled the corpse of their sister and came to the big cliff looking for the body. The witch put a spell on the brothers to make them sleepy...and while the brothers slept the witch dug up their sister's body and took it to her witch cave...a cave where everyone was afraid to go, because the witch lived there. The witch laid the sister's body on a flat stone at the back of the cave...surrounded by bats and snakes and spiders. Then the witch used her potions and magic herbs and brought the sister back to life. The sister opened her eyes slowly and saw the witch and tried to scream but nothing came out of her mouth...no sound.

"But the brothers heard their sister scream in their minds...their thoughts...and they knew she had been taken by a witch and was in bad trouble. So the brothers followed the screams to the witch's cave and planned to kidnap their dead sister who had come back to life. But the witch was on to them, see? She suspected the brothers might try to take their sister back, so the witch cast a spell on the sister and made her life nocturnal. That meant the sister could only live at night. By day she would be dead...just a corpse. But at night she would open her eyes and be alive, like a vampire.

"Not knowing this, the brothers took back their sister that night while she was alive and brought her back to their little adobe house by the big cliff. They hugged and kissed and told stories all night...so glad to be together again. But in the morning they found their sister dead. They cried and cursed the witch, blaming her. Then they buried her again in the same grave and stood watch over her all day. When night came they heard her crying out in the grave...crying for help. So they dug her up again and took her into the house, where she lived with them...except she was dead during the day and alive during the night. I don't know what happened next, because that's where I fell asleep ... the next thing I remember was waking up in the ambulance on my way to the hospital all wrapped up in a sheet...."

Jodie clicked the stop symbol on her recording and looked at Fernando. "So what do you make of that?"

Fernando shrugged. "Lots of tales about witches and shape-shifters in Native and Hispanic folk tales around New Mexico. I don't recall this particular tale, but the elements sound familiar. So what? It's just folklore."

"Just folklore?" Jodie asked. "Our kidnapper doesn't think so."

"Yeah, which is why I have a hard time believing this guy is really a professor of anthropology?" Fernando said. "Maybe we need to make some inquiries at the University of New Mexico."

"Out of my jurisdiction," Jodie said, shaking her head.

Fernando checked his watch. "Well, then, I guess it's on me."

12

Halfway to Albuquerque Fernando remembered how much he hated this drive down Interstate 25. Not even the sight of the Rio Grande as it snaked through Cochiti, Santo Domingo, and San Felipe Pueblo lands relieved his boredom. The outskirts of Albuquerque were even worse because of their ugliness. Factories and industrial areas greeted him as he reduced his speed entering the city limits. He took the Lomas Boulevard Exit east to University Boulevard down to the University of New Mexico campus. From there he followed directions provided by Ruth Johnson, the UNM Department of Anthropology secretary. At Las Lomas he doglegged over to Redondo Drive and then drove a long block south to the Maxwell Museum parking lot, where guests could park at the meters. At first glance the parking lot looked full. Now what would he do?

Taking a chance, Fernando drove through the parking lot and found the last space available. Unfortunately, when he went to plug the meter he found it didn't accept coins, only credit cards. He hated using credit cards in meters. Grumbling, he pulled out his Visa card and stuffed it into the meter. Took him a couple of tries before he learned to operate the damned meter, primarily because he couldn't read the flashing instructions in the bright Albuquerque sun. Finally he got his ticket and placed it on the dashboard of the Cherokee.

According to Ruth, he would find the entrance to the Anthropology Annex Building on the east side of the Maxwell Museum. So he walked around to the eastern side of the museum, ignoring a giant prickly pear cactus that grew as tall as the building. He found the front door under a recessed portico supported by wooden posts with the ends of vigas protruding from its roof. Inside, he walked down a long hallway to the Anthropology Department Office. When he'd called earlier, Ruth penciled him in for a three o'clock meeting with the department chairperson, Doctor Hugh Satterfield. That is, if the good doctor happened to be available. Ruth couldn't say for sure because Satterfield didn't keep regular office hours in the afternoons. Evidently Doctor Hugh Satterfield was a busy man.

Fernando spotted Ruth through the window of the department office. She waved, motioning for him to come into the small office, which he did. "Hi there," she said, a big-haired woman with ratted out hair that curled around her head like a black halo. Her thin bird-like face made her nose seem unusually long, like a beak. "You made it."

"Yeah, thanks to your directions," Fernando said.

"Well, you're in luck. He just came back from a meeting with the dean. He's in his office," Ruth said, pointing to an adjoining room.

Fernando walked to the room and knocked on the half-closed door.

"Come in," a deep voice instructed.

Fernando stepped into the office and found Hugh Satterfield sitting behind a desk literally covered with papers, folders, and books. Satterfield was a large, heavy-set man wearing an old-fashioned three-piece tweed suit that looked totally out of place in the sunny Southwest. His head seemed massive, partly because his jowls hung down below his chin like an old hound dog. His wrinkled face and matted gray hair gave away his age: sixties, probably late sixties.

"Thanks for seeing me on such short notice," Fernando said, taking a seat in the leather chair facing Satterfield's desk.

"No problem, you caught me between meetings," Satterfield chuckled. "Start of the semester is always a busy time for us. So how can I help you?"

"I'm a private investigator working with the Santa Fe County Sheriff on a murder investigation," Fernando said. He went on to explain that authorities had found two women—Gloria Chavez and April Lux—drugged and wrapped in white sheets like mummies at the Cerrillos Hills State Park Visitor Center; that both Gloria and April were pronounced dead, but April seemed to wake up or actually come back to life; and that April described her abductor as a tall, thin man with short black hair and skin as white as milk.

"Okay, but I don't understand how any of this relates to me or this department," Satterfield said, puzzled.

Fernando nodded. "April said her abductor claimed to be an anthropologist at the University of New Mexico."

Satterfield's eyes opened wide. Sighing, he sat back in his chair and ran a hand over his drooping jowls. He seemed to be uncomfortable.

"April also said her abductor talked about witches, which he claimed were real and not just mythology," Fernando added. "That is, he told her about studying and experimenting with witchcraft and the dark arts, if that's the right term."

Now Satterfield looked worried. He shook his head. "Well, I can assure you that none of our faculty fit this description or would ever practice or study witchcraft. However..."

Fernando waited for Satterfield to continue.

The silence made Satterfield even more nervous. He looked around the room, thinking. Then he turned to Fernando and grimaced. "Here's my problem. Academic records are confidential—one might say almost sacrosanct. However, since this matter involves a murder investigation, and since I may be able to help, I feel I have a moral responsibility to share information about one of our past graduate students that might be relevant."

Fernando nodded. "I'm listening."

Satterfield continued. "Last year we had a graduate student who violated our professional standards and, quite frankly, frightened us. His work was dangerous, both theoretically and in practice. Unsound might be a better word. He was obsessed with native tales of cannibalism and witchcraft, including healers who brought people back from the dead. He advocated a kind of immersion forensic anthropology, where the investigator actually lived and practiced what he or she was investigating, whether it be cannibalism or witchcraft related. He had successfully completed our undergraduate Anthropology requirements, but halfway through our graduate Forensic Anthropology research seminar he submitted a paper and proposed a practicum that would, essentially, test the reality of some of these cannibalism and witchcraft stories. That was the final straw. The department voted unanimously to expel him from the program. He appealed our decision, but the dean of the college supported us and expelled the student from the university."

"And you think this might be the man who abducted the two women?" Fernando asked.

"Well, he fits your description—a tall, skinny man with short black hair and a bad complexion, as well as extraordinarily white skin, almost to the degree of an albino."

"What's his name?" Fernando asked.

"His name is Sven Anders. I haven't seen nor heard from him since he left the program," Satterfield said, shaking his head. "Oddly, another student who always came to class with him also disappeared. An undergraduate woman named Melissa Vigil, who was an Anthropology major and one of Anders' students. Anders was a Teaching Assistant in our graduate program, you see; he taught introductory Anthropology classes. I don't know if Miss Vigil was Sven's girlfriend or what, but she always came to class with him and—"

Fernando interrupted Satterfield. "You said Anders frightened you. What did you mean by that?"

Satterfield cleared his throat. "Well, it was his intensity, the way he talked about cannibalism and witchcraft. He seemed—I don't know—almost possessed. He would go on and on about these verboten topics in such a matter-of-fact way that most of our faculty were scared about what he might actually do. We certainly didn't want to endorse or be connected in any way to Anders research. His proposals were unprofessional, unethical, even unhinged."

"Would you happen to have an address for Anders?"

"I don't, but Ruth might. She keeps our student records," Satterfield said. He checked his watch. "I'm sorry, but I have another meeting in five minutes. I'm going to have to cut our conversation short, but hopefully Ruth can answer any other questions you might have."

Fernando handed Satterfield one of his cards. "Thank you. This helps. Please give me a call if you see Anders again or can think of anything else that would help us find him."

Satterfield nodded and then walked to the door. Turning around, he said, "I hope you find him. And if he is responsible for these abductions, I hope he pays for what he has done."

Fernando waved and then followed Satterfield into the department office, where Ruth was already clicking through files on her computer screen. "I heard you talking. Let me see if I can find his address."

It took her only minutes to find Ander's address. "Here," she said, turning the computer monitor so he could see the file with Ander's address in the 300 block of Vassar Drive South.

Fernando copied the address in his pocket notebook and thanked Ruth. He walked quickly out of the Anthropology Annex to his Cherokee in the Maxwell Museum's parking lot. Then he drove down to Central Avenue and turned left, heading for Vassar Drive amid a host of memories, most of them pleasant, from his student days at the university.

13

The house on Vassar Drive turned out to be a 1920s bungalow style adobe, common in the university area. Surrounded by a front yard overgrown with prickly pear and cholla cactus, the adobe had a flat roof and casement windows smothered by heavy curtains inside. Though small, Fernando thought the house looked a bit expensive for a university student to be renting, but what did he know? He hadn't been a student in forty years.

Fernando parked on the street and walked up the sidewalk to the porch. He could hear loud music blaring inside, if you could call it music. More like an angry man shouting out random lyrics without any perceivable melody. He rang the doorbell but didn't hear a bell, so he knocked on the door. Softly at first and then harder, competing with the music. Seconds later the door flew open and he found himself looking into the barrel of a snub-nose pistol.

"Whoa...take it easy," Fernando said, backing up.

"What do you want?" shouted the young man standing in front of him, dressed in black sweats with a Japanese motif headband around his long black hair.

"Uh...are you Sven Anders?" Fernando asked, taken aback by the gun in his face. Did college students carry guns these days? If so, times had certainly changed since he was a college student. Whatever happened to smoking weed and having recreational sex?

The young man lowered his gun. "No, Anders moved out this past Spring. I'm renting the place now."

Fernando nodded. "Do you happen to know where he moved to?"

"No, but you can ask him yourself, he's out back getting his shit out of the garage," the young man said, waving his gun in the general direction of the garage. "Fucker was supposed to have it out months ago."

"No kidding?" Fernando asked, noticing the driveway beside the house. "Thanks. I will."

"And tell him to get all of his stuff out of the garage today or I'll throw it out on the street tomorrow for the garbage truck," the young man said.

Fernando saluted and then walked around to the driveway. He saw a beat-up Toyota Tacoma pickup parked in front of the garage, its once red color faded to a motley orange. The bed of the pickup had been loaded with boxes of books and household items, as well as a few pieces of furniture, notably chairs and a small end table. He saw no sign of Anders as he approached the garage, an old-fashioned garage with large double doors that opened manually. Next to the doors he spotted several more boxes waiting to be loaded in the pickup.

Feeling vulnerable, Fernando stopped to take a look around. He wished he'd brought his Smith & Wesson. He'd left the pistol back in his office, not expecting to need it at the university. Big mistake.

"Anders? Are you here?" he asked loudly.

No response, so Fernando moved slowly toward the open garage doors. He saw only shadows inside the dark, windowless interior. Now that the sun had set behind the garage, the only light inside came from the open doors behind him. Entering the dark garage, he smelled the strong odor of oil and gasoline. As his eyes adjusted to the darkness he could make out a workbench at the rear of the building and a tangle of yard tools leaning against the wall. And something else on the bench. Maybe a chainsaw.

Suddenly he heard a shuffling sound behind him. Was Anders coming into the garage? He started to turn around, but too late. A wooden chair hit him from behind and sent him careening to the floor.

Bright colors flashed behind his eyes as he landed on top of a cardboard box, dazed.

The back of his head throbbed with pain. His shoulders felt numb, as if both collar bones had been broken. He rolled over on his back, trying to maintain consciousness. His wobbly vision made him dizzy. While he struggled to see, the double doors swung closed, plunging the garage into darkness. Then he heard the dry click of a padlock outside on the door.

Fernando lay on the flat of his back, trying to gather his strength. When he breathed the pain in his ribs was nearly unbearable. He felt the back of his throbbing head but found no blood, just a lump the size of his fist. He took a few deep breaths and then lay still, breathing slowly in and out. Trying to relax.

After a few minutes he managed to sit up and take stock of his situation. Fragments of the chair that had beaned him littered the floor. A rattan chair. Luckily it wasn't solid oak or metal. Even so, he didn't feel so damned lucky.

He stretched his arms and shoulders to make sure nothing was broken. Then he tried to stand up. The first try landed him back on his ass, so he tried again. This time he maintained his balance long enough to stagger over to the double doors. He tried to open the doors, but as he suspected Anders had padlocked the doors from the outside. The sonofabitch.

Head pounding, he moved carefully, mindfully over to the pedestrian door, only to find it also locked. Not giving up, he stumbled through a minefield of gas cans, garbage cans, and assorted trash to the yard tools near the workbench. He found rakes, shovels, weed wackers, and an axe leaning against the wall. He chose the axe and took it to the pedestrian door and began smashing the lock. He worked furiously, hacking at the door until the door sprung back at him, smacking him in the knee. He cursed and flung the axe as hard as he could behind him. The axe clanked and rattled and smashed against something metal.

"Hey—what the fuck?" someone shouted from the back porch of the house. The young man he'd seen in the house came running out to the garage, waving his pistol in front of him.

Out of patience, Fernando snarled. "Son, if you don't put that fucking pistol away, I'm gonna take it away from you and beat you with it."

Taken aback, the young man stuffed the gun in his waistband. "Jesus, what happened to you?" he asked.

"Anders," Fernando said and pushed the punk out of his way, heading for his Cherokee. Still wobbly on his feet.

The young man glanced into the garage and started cursing. "He didn't take all his shit with him. If he comes back here again, I'll shoot the fucker for you," he called after Fernando.

"Help yourself," Fernando said, climbing in the Cherokee. He opened the glove compartment to get his emergency bottle of Advil and popped a couple of tablets. Then he sat there for a few minutes, waiting for his blurry vision to disappear. When it did, sort of, he drove back to Central Avenue and down to the Frontier Restaurant, which he remembered from his student days. He found a parking place on a side street and walked into the restaurant.

All eyes watched him walk unsteadily over to one of the back tables and sit down. Only when he sat down did he feel the wetness on the back of his neck. So he was bleeding. Not good.

One of the young servers came right over, a punky looking woman with red-streaked hair and a ring in her nose. "Are you okay?" she asked.

Her question confused Fernando at first, but then he realized he must look like the walking dead. His shirt was soiled and ripped in back, his face and hands were smudged with oil and dirt, and he had a lump on the side of his head the size of an orange. Either walking dead or a homeless person, what else could they think?

"Oh, yeah...sorry, I took a fall," Fernando said, trying to put the best face on his situation.

The punky young woman looked at him skeptically. "Can I get you something?"

"Green chile cheeseburger, fries, water, and lots of coffee," Fernando rattled off, a little too fast. So fast he sounded desperate.

She gave him the Evil Eye but wrote down his order and then immediately brought him a glass of water and a cup of coffee. The coffee helped. He started to perk up when the caffeine kicked in, that and the Advil. He took his time eating his meal, trying to delay the long drive back to Santa Fe until he felt up to the task. By the time he finished and walked out of the Frontier the sun had long since set in the western sky. For a moment he forgot where he'd parked the Cherokee, but streetlights along Central Avenue guided him to the correct side street.

Behind the wheel, Fernando drove down Central Avenue and turned right onto the ramp to I-25 North to Santa Fe. He drove five miles per hour under the speed limit, just to be on the safe side.

Over an hour later he pulled into his driveway on Acequia Madre Street. He didn't see Estelle's Camry in the garage. So he went inside the house and took a quick shower, disinfecting the wound on the back of his head. Then he tossed his dirty clothing in the trash and went directly to bed.

14

Fernando tossed and turned most of the night, mostly because he couldn't get comfortable. His head throbbed and his back hurt like a motherfucker. When he got out of bed around Midnight to take another Advil, he noticed Estelle sleeping on the other side of their bed. He hadn't heard her come in last night, but it must have been late. He climbed back in bed and waited for the Advil to kick in, which seemed to take longer the more capsules he popped. Round about two o'clock he got up to pee and popped another Advil for good measure. He must have slept finally, because when he heard Estelle making their morning coffee in the kitchen he felt somewhat rested, if groggy. Then again he was always groggy in the morning before coffee.

Climbing out from under the bed-sheets, he took his time sitting on the edge of the bed to get his bearings. The good news was that his headache had devolved into a dull ache. The bad news was that his back hurt every time he moved, which was constantly. He felt the back of his head and found the swelling, about the size of a golf ball now. Apparently he'd over-estimated his injury last night.

Clenching his teeth, Fernando got up and went into the master bath. He rummaged through their medicine cabinet until he found the tube of Ted's Pain Cream that Estelle used for her arthritis. He smeared the cream on his shoulders and back, as far down as he could reach, and then got dressed. He didn't like what he saw in the bathroom mirror: dark shadows under his eyes, deep wrinkles in his forehead. He looked tired and in pain, which was exactly how he felt.

Once dressed, he made his way to the kitchen where Estelle was already eating breakfast. She looked at him suspiciously and asked, "Where were you last night? You missed Fidel's memorial celebration."

Fernando shook his head. "I know. I got tied up in Albuquerque on business."

Estelle frowned. "He was one of your best friends."

She seemed about to berate him but then noticed his head. "Wait...what happened to your head?" She came over to feel his lump.

"Yeah, I had a little accident," Fernando said. "It's nothing, really."

"Uh-huh. You're supposed to be retired, remember?" Estelle asked.

They went back and forth on whether Fernando should be completely, once and for all, retired. The same discussion they'd had a hundred times before. Finally Estelle took her lunch out of the refrigerator and left for work at the Saint Francis Immigrant Outreach Program.

Alone, enjoying the peace and quiet, Fernando made himself a hot breakfast of eggs and sausage with a healthy dash of red chile. He drank a second cup of coffee and then did some light exercises, stretching his muscles. He found the more he moved the better his bruised muscles and bones felt. Loosened up, that is. They still ached, just not as badly.

He was about to leave for his office when his cell phone rang. After the last couple of days his first instinct was to toss the damn phone in the trash. He didn't. Instead, he sat down at the kitchen table and glanced at the name of the caller.

"I've got an idea," Jodie said, not bothering to identify herself.

Fernando laughed. "Well, I have more than an idea. I have some news."

"Shoot," Jodie said.

"I know the identity of our abductor," Fernando said. "I had a run-in with him in Albuquerque yesterday afternoon."

"Seriously?" Jodie asked.

"Seriously," Fernando said. "I talked to the chair of the Anthropology Department at the University of New Mexico, Hugh Satterfield. I gave him April's description of her abductor, including his claim to be a professor of anthropology. Satterfield knew right away who it was—a former anthropology graduate student who they expelled because of his obsession with witchcraft and cannibalism. Apparently the student even attempted to practice witchcraft as part of his research. The student's name is Sven Anders."

"So that's the foreign sounding name...like April mentioned," Jodie said.

"Exactly," Fernando said. "The department secretary gave me the address they had on file for Anders, so I paid him a little visit. Turned out someone else was renting the house when I got there, but I found Anders out back removing some of his belongings stored in the garage. I didn't actually get to talk to him because the sonofabitch surprised me and hit me over the head from behind. With a chair. Then he locked me in the garage and drove away before I could get out."

"Jesus...did you have to go to the emergency room?"

"No, it was a fairly light rattan chair," Fernando said. "I just have a knot on the back of my head. And my shoulders hurt from falling on a bunch of boxes."

"Did you get his license number, at least?" Jodie asked.

"No, everything happened so fast, I just didn't think of it in time," Fernando said. "He drove a faded red Toyota Tacoma pickup, maybe five to ten years old."

"Well, that's something," Jodie said.

"Yeah, so we know his name and what he's driving," Fernando added.

"But we don't know the location of his Cerrillos pit house, or whatever it's called," Jodie came back. "Which is why I'm calling. I have an idea how we can find this place."

"I'm listening," Fernando said.

"Okay...what if we set a trap?" Jodie asked. "Have one of our female officers hang out at the hotel bars downtown. You know, waiting for this Anders guy to hit on her. We would send her out with a GPS Tracker. That way we could follow her to this place in Cerrillos and catch Anders red-handed. What do you think?"

Fernando laughed. "What are you saying? You plan to dress up like a hooker and hang out at the bars?"

Jodie sounded offended. "Hah! That's a laugh. I'm not exactly the type of woman who picks up men. You know that, right? I intimidate most men. And for good reason."

"Yes you do," Fernando agreed.

"Except you," Jodie said.

"Well, that's because I'm used to strong women," Fernando said. "My mother was tough as nails, a true matriarch. So's my wife, though that's different because we're married."

Jodie laughed. "You're too cranky to be intimidated, Fernando."

Now Fernando laughed too. "You're probably right. So who do you have in mind then?"

"Do you remember Laura Ortega?" Jodie asked. "She came on board about a year ago. She's willing to do it. And she looks the type, what you men call 'hot.' So what do you think?"

Fernando considered for a long moment. "I don't know, it could be dangerous to leave her alone with Anders for any length of time. And how do we abort if something goes wrong?"

"Okay, what if I bring Laura down to your office this afternoon?" Jodie asked. "Say about one o'clock? We can talk about it more. The three of us."

As usual, Jodie clicked off before Fernando could respond. He could tell she had already made up her mind to go through with this scheme, come hell or high water. He had to wonder if it was worth the risk.

15

Fernando brooded all morning. He worried about putting a police officer in harm's way. Wouldn't Anders recognize the plant? Surely most people, including Anders, would not confuse a female police officer with a hooker. And if the plan went awry, how would they rescue the officer? Was the payoff worth risking Laura's life? There must be a better way, he kept thinking. But what?

Troubled, Fernando decided he'd try to talk Jodie out of going through with the plan. That wouldn't be easy, given Jodie's headstrong nature. Maybe he could enlist the support of Laura Ortega, whom he'd never met. Surely Laura must have some doubts about going into a murderer's den all by her lonesome.

After lunch, he locked up the house and climbed into his Cherokee. He drove around the Paseo to Canyon Road and up to his office. He found several cars parked near Ruby's gallery, so he pulled up in front of his Private Eye sign. He walked down the gravel path to his office and opened the door, replacing the 'Closed' sign with his 'Open' sign. The light on his answering machine blinked at him as he walked to his desk and sat down.

Two messages. The first from a kid who wanted help finding his dog, which Fernando deleted. The second from a woman who claimed she was being stalked and wanted protection. He jotted down the woman's phone number on a legal pad and was about to call her back when he heard the crunching of gravel on the path leading to his office. Someone approached his door. When the door opened without a knock, he knew it was Jodie, who never knocked. Behind Jodie came Laura Ortega, with auburn-colored hair down to her shoulders and gray-green eyes that sparkled.

That first glimpse of Laura changed Fernando's mind about Jodie's plan. Not only was Laura drop dead gorgeous, she had a naughty, ironic smile that any man would find irresistible.

"This is Laura," Jodie said, by way of introduction. "Laura, Fernando Lopez. He helps us out from time to time."

Laura smiled. "Nice to finally meet you, Fernando. I heard a lot about you when you were chief detective."

Fernando laughed. "Good things, I hope."

Laura laughed too. "Mostly."

"Have a seat," Fernando said, bringing a second chair over to the desk.

"So we need a plan," Jodie said to Fernando.

Ignoring Jodie for the moment, Fernando turned to Laura and asked, "Do you really want to go through with this?"

"I do," Laura said, looking him in the eye. "Let me tell you why. I live out in Cuyamungue, near Tesuque pueblo, where last spring a woman was raped and murdered and tossed in the town dump. You might have read about it in the *Independent*. That woman was my best friend. She was a single mother raising two small kids by herself, because her ex-husband was an irresponsible drunk and womanizer. Those kids are living with their grandparents now. Those of us who knew her are left with the image of a naked woman with an electric cord wrapped around her neck lying in a mountain of garbage."

Fernando did not immediately respond. He vaguely remembered the case. No one had ever been charged with the murder, as far as he knew.

"I'm so tired of men and their violence against women," Laura said. "Dozens of native and Hispanic women are raped and murdered each year in this state, hundreds across the country. Men who murder women and children need to be locked up—or eliminated, I don't care which. Remember the West Mesa murders in Albuquerque? The bodies of eleven women were found there in 2009, all of them murdered. And to this day no one was been charged with the crimes. Think of it, eleven women, and the murder or murderers have never been caught. So yeah, I want to eliminate this asshole, this guy who's abducting and killing women in Santa Fe. I'm willing to do everything in my power."

Fernando nodded.

"And don't worry, I can take care of myself," Laura said.

Jodie was beaming. She turned to Fernando, "You see, I chose well."

"Yes, you did," Fernando said. "And I agree. Whoever's doing this needs to be stopped, one way or another. But you're right, we need a plan."

"Jodie's told me all about this Sven Anders guy," Laura said. "So here's our plan. I'll dress up like a hooker, wear a racy dress and lots of makeup. I'll start at the Hilton bar and then, if I don't see him there, I'll walk over to the bar at La Fonda. If he hasn't shown up by ten o'clock or so, we'll call it quits and try again the following night. You'll know I've given up when I head for the parking lot on Washington Avenue. I'll have the GPS tracker inside my hair brooch...it's a large sterling silver brooch. So if he does show up and I leave with him, you'll be able to track my movements from the bar to wherever he takes me."

"We can do that," Fernando said.

"Yeah, I'll have my laptop in the cruiser," Jodie said. "We'll park downtown and be waiting, say from about seven o'clock to ten, if that's when you want to quit. As soon as you leave the bar, we'll be up and running. We'll follow as close as we can without being too obvious. But be careful, it's a long dark highway to Cerrillos, especially on the deserted roads around Devil's Throne. He could stop anywhere along the way and try to assault you."

Fernando nodded. "Yeah, it's tricky, because there's lots of dirt roads he could pull off on. If he switched off his lights, we could have trouble finding you."

Laura shrugged. "If that happens, I'll just have to fend for myself."

"When do we start?" Fernando asked.

"Tonight," Jodie said. "Why wait until another woman is abducted?"

With that, they agreed to be in place at seven o'clock that night, Laura at the Hilton and Fernando and Jodie in her cruiser downtown. Laura saluted as she walked out of his office. Jodie stopped and turned back to Fernando. "I'll pick you up here quarter till seven, okay?"

"I'll be here," Fernando said.

Alone, Fernando debated what to do next. Then he remembered the message on his machine about the stalker. The woman who'd left the message identified herself as Mary Moore. He found her number on his legal pad and dialed, on the off chance her stalker might be the Cuyamungue murderer Laura mentioned or, even less likely, Sven Anders.

"Mary Moore," she answered immediately.

"This is Fernando Lopez, returning your call," he said. "I understand you're being harassed by a stalker. Is that right?"

"Oh...thanks for getting back to me so quickly," she said. "Yes, he's been bothering me for a couple of months now. It's gotten to the point where I'm starting to worry. I'm afraid of him."

"You should be afraid, these people can be dangerous," Fernando said. "Do you have any idea who this person is?"

"Yes, Bob Peters, he works at City Hall with me," she said. "Well, not exactly with me, he's an assessor in the property tax division, I'm in the IT department. We went out once, just for drinks, because he kept bugging me. Since then I've made it clear to him that I'm not interested, but he keeps after me. Following me. He even comes over to my house and parks in the driveway. Just sits in his car, waiting for me to come out, I guess. He might have mental issues, I don't know."

"I see," Fernando said. "Well, here's what you should do. Report the stalker to the police right away. Get a restraining order on Peters. You probably won't need a lawyer, but if you do, call Raoul Garcia, he's the best lawyer in Santa Fe. Tell him Fernando sent you."

"Do you really think I need to get the police involved?" she asked.

"Yes, because stalking is a misdemeanor," Fernando said. "Aggravated as in repeated stalking is a fourth-degree felony. You need to take this seriously, because these guys can be violent."

Silence at the other end of the line. "Okay, I'll report it to the police," she said reluctantly.

"And listen, if this guy keeps on stalking you or tries to make any kind of physical contact, call me immediately," Fernando said. "I'll come right over and take care of him. It would be my pleasure. Seriously."

16

After an early dinner, Fernando told Estelle he had an appointment with a client and drove down to his office at half past six o'clock. He wore an open carry holster that held his Smith & Wesson, intending to be well prepared if they encountered Sven Anders. He had a score to settle with Anders and payback time had arrived. If Anders went for the bait, they would follow him to his lair and nail his ass. Anders could try to practice his witchcraft in the Big House. Wouldn't the other cons love that?

He heard Jodie drive into the parking lot at a quarter till seven, as punctual as always. Locking up his office, he went out to meet her. He was surprised to find her sitting in the front passenger's seat with the overhead light turned on. He walked over to the passenger's side of the cruiser and opened her door. When he did, he saw Jodie holding her laptop and cell phone in her lap. "You're driving," she said. "I'm handling the electronics."

Fernando nodded, walking around the cruiser and climbing into the driver's seat. He felt right at home, even if he hadn't driven a fully loaded cruiser since retiring from the Santa Fe Police Department two years ago. He drove over to Delgado Street and then down East Alameda Street past the Paseo. On Cathedral Place he found a parking spot located next to La Fonda and only five short blocks from the Hilton. This would be a perfect place from which to monitor Laura's movements from both the Hilton and La Fonda.

Jodie cracked open her laptop and zeroed in on Laura's GPS Tracker, currently at the Hilton. They watched for over an hour without seeing any movement. Then, just after eight o'clock, Laura left the Hilton.

"She's moving—get ready," Jodie said. "I don't know, she may have hooked up with Anders."

They watched Laura's movement as she walked up San Francisco Street. After a couple of blocks it became apparent to them that Laura was headed toward the La Fonda Hotel.

"Damn, Anders wasn't at the Hilton," Jodie said. "She's going to try the La Fonda Bar."

Sure enough, they watched the cursor move to La Fonda and stop. Again they watched and waited for what seemed like hours. So long that Fernando's back began to bark. He climbed out of the cruiser to stretch his muscles. Getting back in he heard Jodie curse and close her laptop.

"Not going to happen tonight," Jodie said. "She's giving up. She's headed for the parking lot on Washington Avenue, just like she said she would when she was giving up for the night."

Jodie stepped out of the cruiser and placed her laptop in the back seat. Then she motioned for Fernando to move over to the passenger's seat. He followed her directions, riding shotgun as she started the cruiser and made a U-turn on Cathedral Place. They drove back to Fernando's office in silence. When Jodie dropped him off, she said, "We'll try again tomorrow. I'll pick you up at the same time."

Fernando saluted as she took off down Canyon Road. He climbed into his Cherokee and drove around the Paseo to Acequia Madre, which was dark and deserted at this hour. Not a pedestrian or a vehicle on the street. When he pulled into their driveway he saw a light in their bedroom at the rear of the house. Estelle must have waited up for him. Unusual for Estelle, who liked to be in bed by nine o'clock at the latest so she could get an early start the next day at her nonprofit. She was definitely a morning person, unlike Fernando, who never completely woke up until at least ten o'clock, sometimes Noon.

He parked next to the garage, where Estelle kept her precious Camry. She loved that car even more than he loved his Cherokee. Fernando had no idea why. A sedan was a sedan, end of story.

Walking through the garden, he noticed leaves from the tall cottonwood trees that bordered their land had begun to fall on the patio. That time of year, with the autumn chill soon to come, followed by the winter cold. Yes, Santa Fe could get damn cold in the winter.

He unlocked the door and stepped into a dark kitchen.

"That you, Fernando?" Estelle called from the master bedroom.

"Yes, I'll be there in a second," Fernando said.

He removed his holster and placed it on a shelf in his study. Then he walked back to the bedroom, where Estelle had propped herself up in bed reading a dog-eared copy of John Nichols' *The Milagro Beanfield War*.

Fernando laughed. "How many times have you read that?"

"This is the third time," Estelle said. "I think it gets even better the more times you read it."

"Whatever you say."

"So are you going to tell me what you're working on all hours of the day and night?" Estelle asked, putting her book aside. "I'd like to know. I am, after all, your wife. Remember?"

Fernando sighed. "It's a long story."

"I'm listening," Estelle said.

So Fernando told her the whole story, from the appearance of the first mummy woman, who was dead, to the discovery of the second mummy woman, who was dead but came back to life, to his work identifying Sven Anders as the man who abducted the women and the man who murdered Fidel, who was investigating the disappearance of the first woman. Now their focus was on finding Anders, who apparently lived somewhere around Cerrillos. Near Devil's Throne.

Fernando chose not to mention all the rumors and innuendo about Anders' involvement in witchcraft. He didn't want to muddy the waters. Plus it would be damn difficult to explain just what Anders was trying to do with his so-called witchcraft—if, that is, Fernando even knew.

Estelle listened without making a comment.

"At the moment we're trying to trap Anders," Fernando added. "One of the female officers at the sheriff's office is dressing like a hooker and hanging out at the hotels where Anders has picked up the women he's abducted. She's wearing a GPS Tracker, so we can follow her to wherever he's hiding. We hope. That's the plan, anyway."

"That's where you were tonight?" Estelle asked.

Fernando nodded. "We'll try again tomorrow night."

Pausing, Estelle stared at Fernando. "Well, I'm pleased to hear you're working to stop violence against women, I don't care what their situation or profession happens to be. I can't tell you how many horror stories I hear every day, working for the Immigrant Outreach Program. We're told that somewhere between sixty and eighty percent of the women from Central America crossing the border from Mexico have been sexually assaulted on their journey north. I know the numbers of native women raped and murdered every year are just horrible, but I think the situation with migrant women might be even worse. The numbers are staggering."

By the time Fernando climbed into bed Estelle had placed her book on the bedside table and turned off the light. Dog tired, he fell asleep immediately, only to plunge into a troubled, terrifying world of nightmares.

Dreaming, he walked into a semi-dark building of deepening shadows. Suddenly something hard hit his head from behind and he pitched forward into the shadows, landing on his face. He groped around on the concrete floor and felt a soft object warm to the touch. When he got to his knees he discovered the warm object was a mummy wrapped in white cloth squirming on the floor. He could tell it was a woman because of its shape. Panicking, he ripped at the white cloth, trying to unwind the cloth so the woman could breath. The more cloth he removed the more immobile the woman became until she stopped moving altogether. She'd stopped breathing—she was dying! He tore off the last shred of cloth and looked down at the face of his oldest daughter, Flavia.

"Help! Help!" Fernando screamed, waking Estelle in the bed next to him.

"What? What's the matter?" Estelle asked, sitting up in bed.

Fernando realized he'd been having a nightmare. Flavia wasn't a mummy. She wasn't dying in his arms.

"Just a nightmare," Fernando said. "Sorry."

Estelle sighed and slid back down, pulling the blankets over her head.

Fernando reached for the bottle of sleeping pills he kept on his nightstand. He hated to take them, but he needed to sleep. Desperately.

17

Fernando woke up late with a foggy head. Sleeping pills always left him feeling numb and confused. It usually took him an hour or so to clear his head. He stumbled into the bathroom and took a hot shower, which helped some but not enough. After dressing, he shuffled to the kitchen to make himself breakfast. Estelle had left him half a pot of coffee before departing for her job with the outreach program, so he poured himself a cup and heated it in the microwave. He found a leftover enchilada in the refrigerator, which he didn't bother to heat before wolfing it down in three bites. Then he made himself a piece of toast with cherry jam and sat down at the kitchen table with a second cup of coffee.

Brooding, he reflected on last night's events, or lack of events. He didn't know how many more nights he could stand to sit in a cramped car with Jodie for three hours. He liked and respected Jodie, but she tended to be a bit too intense for his taste, too severe. All business, all the time. A great cop, but not the easiest person to spend time with. He figured he could manage one more night, maybe two, but after that Jodie would have to find someone else.

His head started to clear after the second cup of coffee, so Fernando poured himself a third. Just as he sat back down at the kitchen table his cell phone rang. He expected Jodie but was surprised to see Manny Alvarez's name on the screen. Usually when Manny called it meant one of two things: happy hour at El Farol, or bad news. Since it was way too early for happy hour, Fernando expected the worst. He wasn't disappointed.

"Hey, Fernando, I could use your help. Do you have a few minutes?" Manny asked.

"Sure, what's up?"

"We have a homicide up on Don Gaspar Avenue," Manny said. " Middle-aged woman—looks like she was strangled. We found your name and phone number written on a pad next to her land line."

Fernando's spirits sank.

"Her name's Mary Moore," Manny said. "Any idea why she had your name and contact information beside her phone. Do you know her?"

Fernando sighed, then cursed. "She called me yesterday, said she had a stalker following her. I told her to call the police and get a restraining order. Fuck!"

"Yeah, she never called," Manny said.

"I should have done more," Fernando said, his mood darkening. "I should have gotten involved. Goddamnit!"

"How 'bout you tell me all about it," Manny said.

"Okay. Where are you?" Fernando asked.

"I'm at her house on Don Gaspar, just a couple of blocks before Cordova Road," Manny said, and gave him the street address.

"I'm on my way," Fernando said and clicked off.

He filled a thermos with the remaining coffee and grabbed his holster before heading out. He locked his Smith & Wesson in the glove compartment of the Cherokee and then drove down to the Paseo and around to Don Gaspar. Lined with expensive houses, the broad, well-maintained avenue looked glorious in the early morning light. The light usually cheered Fernando, no matter how tired or groggy he happened to be, but not today. He had gone to the dark place.

Mary Moore's house turned out to be a small, Territorial-style structure with tall windows and a large yard partially hidden behind an adobe wall. Fernando pulled into the short drive and marveled at the exquisitely manicured yard, with flowerbeds and shrubbery surrounding the house. He found Manny's cruiser parked behind a gray Volvo station wagon. He pulled up behind the cruiser and set the brake on the Cherokee. Apparently the Forensics van hadn't arrived yet, which would give him time to talk to Manny and look around by himself.

Fernando followed the sidewalk around to the front door, which was wide open. He spotted Manny inside, standing at the end of a long hallway. When Fernando opened the screen door and stepped inside, Manny turned to greet him.

"Back here," Manny said, a short, wiry forty-year-old with thinning black hair.

Fernando walked through a small living area crowded with an overstuffed sofa and chairs gathered around a coffee table. Bookshelves and oil paintings lined the walls of the upscale, well-furnished house. He joined Manny, who waited for him in the door to a back bedroom. As Fernando approached, Manny stepped to the side, revealing the contents of the bedroom.

Face down on the tousled bed lay the lifeless body of Mary Moore, her skirt hiked up over her bare bottom. An overturned lamp on the bedside table and a scattering of objects on the carpeted floor showed evidence of a struggle.

"Looks like she was strangled, from the marks on her neck," Manny said. "Forensics should be here soon."

Fernando examined the bruises on the woman's neck and the traces of blood on the bedspread. Once again he felt overwhelmed by the guilt and regret that had plagued him for the past thirty-some years. He should have done more when Mary Moore called and asked for his help. He should have known she wouldn't be likely to call the police and get a restraining order on a co-worker. He did know. So why didn't he offer to help her? Why had he been so goddamn passive?

"So what did Mary Moore say when she called?" Manny asked. "Did she know her stalker?"

Fernando nodded. "He's a co-worker, Bob Peters. They both work at City Hall, her in the IT department, and he as a property tax assessor. She said they'd gone out once and ever since Peters had been stalking her. Wouldn't take no for an answer. Sometimes he would park at the end of the driveway and just stare at her house. Like I said, I told her to call the police and get a restraining order.'

"Did she say anything about Peters being violent?" Manny asked.

"No, I guess that's why I wasn't worried about an immediate threat," Fernando answered.

"Yeah...you didn't know," Manny said, not very convincingly.

"What do you want to do?" Fernando asked.

Manny thought for a moment. "I'll wait until Forensics finishes here, gathering whatever evidence they can. Then I'll bring in Peters for fingerprinting and a DNA test. My guess is that Miguel and Teresa will find Peters' fingerprints and DNA all over the bedroom. Looks like a crime of passion to me. Should be easy to round up Peters."

Fernando nodded. "I'll get out of your way, then."

Manny waved.

Shaking his head, Fernando walked out of the house and headed for his Cherokee. He had to admit Manny had become a damn good detective. That was the only positive thing he could say about this godforsaken day. Manny had outgrown his youthful, smart-ass sense of humor. Losing a kidney and part of his large intestine to a Sinaloa Cartel gunman tended to have a definite sobering effect.

Fernando knew Manny would take care of Bob Peters.

18

Still shaken, Fernando sat in his office brooding about how he could have helped Mary Moore. He was haunted by bad memories, by the ghosts of those he could or should have helped but didn't. It came with the territory, as he well knew, but after thirty-some years the ghosts had so multiplied that he couldn't get them out of his head, no matter how he tried. Estelle claimed he was clinically depressed and would remain clinically depressed until he left the profession altogether. Nice thought, but he wasn't naïve enough to think the bad memories would simply disappear. The ghosts would never leave him—he understood that now. Accepted it, more or less, because what choice did he have?

After what happened to Mary Moore, Fernando decided he couldn't very well abandon Jodie, no matter how many hours they had to sit in the cruiser waiting for Sven Anders to take the bait. He would just have to suck it up tonight and however many nights it took to catch Anders in their trap. So he prepared the same as before, eating an early dinner at home without Estelle, who was still at work, and then coming back to his office. The only thing he did differently was to grab a can of Modelo out of his mini-refrigerator when he walked out to meet Jodie.

Jodie frowned when she saw him climbing into her cruiser with a can of beer. "So are you drinking on the job now?"

"I'm not on the job, you are," Fernando said. "I'm only helping out."

Jodie gave him the Evil Eye. "Whatever. But I'm not letting you drive holding a can of beer."

So instead, Jodie drove downtown and this time parked on Alameda Street. Then they changed seats, Jodie moving to the passenger's seat with her laptop and cell phone and Fernando sitting behind the wheel.

Just after seven o'clock the action started.

"Okay...got her," Jodie said. "She's entering the Hilton now."

Fernando relaxed. He opened his can of Modelo and took a long drink. Much better. He should have done this last night. Maybe bring two beers in the future. Just to make the wait a bit more tolerable.

Jodie studied her laptop, while Fernando drank his Modelo and occasionally checked his cell phone for messages. The first hour went by without incident. Then it began.

"Wait…Laura's moving," Jodie said suddenly, a few minutes past eight o'clock. "She's on Guadalupe Street traveling south, not going to La Fonda."

Fernando peered over her shoulder, trying to see. They waited impatiently, silently.

Suddenly Jodie burst out with "Yes! Now she's on Cerrillos Road!"

"Anders took the bait," Fernando said, putting away his cell phone and starting the cruiser. He waited for Jodie's instructions.

"Now they've turned on State Road Fourteen heading to Cerrillos," Jodie said. "Let's go! Don't let them get too far ahead."

Fernando pulled out from their parking space and drove down Alameda Street to South Guadalupe, falling further behind Anders and Laura. He missed the stoplight on Cerrillos Road, which slowed them down even more. They'd miscalculated, it was proving much more difficult to catch up with Anders than they thought. If only they'd parked somewhere on Cerrillos Road and watched for Anders.

Too late now. By the time they made it to the off-ramp to State Road 14 Anders was halfway to the town of Cerrillos.

"Can't you drive any faster?" Jodie asked. "We're losing them."

"I'm going as fast as I can," Fernando said. He shot Jodie a dirty glance, doing the best he could to navigate the winding two-lane highway through the dark countryside that seemed to close in on them as they left the city limits. Only their headlights and the momentary flicker of a yard light from a distant farm or ranch kept the darkness from swallowing them.

"What? Something's wrong," Jodie said. "The signal stopped moving."

"Where?" Fernando asked.

"In Cerrillos," Jodie said.

Fernando slowed down. "But April said his house was a good distance outside of town, near Devil's Throne."

"Now it's moving again!" Jodie shouted, getting more excited by the minute. "It's moving northeast of Cerrillos toward Waldo. No, it stopped again. Looks like it stopped at Devil's Throne."

"Makes no sense," Fernando said, confused. "Why would Anders stop at Devil's Throne?"

Jodie did not respond.

Fernando turned onto the blacktop leading into Cerrillos and drove through a sprinkling of faint lights. He passed the Cerrillos State Park Visitor Center and then followed the dirt road that wound its way through the dark mesa toward Devil's Throne. Up ahead the cruiser's headlights splashed on ghostly rock formations and gnarly juniper and piñon trees, their twisted branches resembling arms reaching out of the darkness to grab at them.

Climbing the last rise, Fernando pulled up facing the nearly vertical front of Devil's Throne. The top of the huge andesite rock glistened in the moonlight. He wasn't sure, but he thought he saw something moving on top, so he left their headlights on so they could see to search the area around Devil's Throne.

"Be careful," Jodie said, stepping out of the cruiser and moving forward with her service pistol in hand.

Fernando took his Smith & Wesson out of its holster and circled around behind the big rock. He crept slowly out of the headlight beams and into the shadows. Puzzled, he didn't see Anders' red Toyota pickup, nor did he see Anders. He noticed the back of Devil's Throne was sloped and jagged, not vertical like the front. He scanned the slope looking for the GPS tracking device, which had to be around here somewhere, either thrown on the rock or left on the ground somewhere nearby. Feeling a sense of urgency, he searched frantically for the tracking device. His greatest fear: that Laura may be alone with Anders and in some distress.

No luck. He couldn't see a damned thing in the darkness behind Devil's Throne. Giving up, he circled around to the front of the rock looking for Jodie.

Jodie stood halfway between the cruiser and Devil's Throne. "What's that?" she asked, pointing west toward an arroyo.

Fernando strained his eyes, looking for whatever Jodie had seen. Looked like something, human or animal, was moving out of the darkness toward them. Anders?

Fernando raised his Smith & Wesson. "Who's there?"

"Hey," a faint voice called out. "It's me."

"Must be Laura," Jodie said, excitement in her voice. She walked out to meet the missing woman.

Fernando stayed behind, hearing the two women talking. Then he watched them materialize out of the darkness, walking slowly toward him. Jodie had her arm around Laura, who limped along beside her. When they came closer Fernando saw Laura's dress had been torn in front, revealing her undergarments. Her upper lip was split and the left side of her face was badly swollen. She looked as though she'd just left the ring of a UFC match.

Jodie helped Laura to the cruiser. The injured woman plopped down in the front passenger's seat with her legs hanging out the door. She made no effort to move her legs into the cruiser.

"What happened?" Jodie asked.

Laura sighed. "He figured out I was a cop...I guess by the questions I was asking. He drove me behind the rock and started mauling me in his truck. I managed to elbow him in the face and open my door. Then I jumped out and tried to run, but he caught me and slapped me across the face several times. Finally I wrestled out of his grip and kicked him in the crotch. When he bent over, I ran as best I could over to the arroyo and hid. Stayed very quiet. He came looking for me after a while, but it was too dark, so he gave up and drove away."

"What happened to the GPS Tracker?" Jodie asked.

"I don't know, I lost it when we were fighting," Laura said. "On the ground somewhere."

"Which way did he go when he drove off?" Fernando asked.

"I think west toward Waldo and Interstate Twenty-Five," Laura said. "Although I'm not sure. It's hard to tell directions when you're punch drunk and hiding in a dark arroyo."

"What else did you find out?" Jodie asked.

"Well, for one thing, he's stronger than he looks," Laura said. "He may be skinny, but he's tall and wiry. And angry. He complained about his anthropology professors at UNM, said they'd kicked him out of school and ruined his career. Called them sheep, too afraid of his research to consider his theories about medicinal herbs and witchcraft tales, which he claimed were real, not just tall tales or mythology. He was convinced he'd been wronged by the establishment, as he called it, and swore that he would get his revenge on the department and prove everyone wrong."

"Did he mention any of the other women he's abducted for his so-called research?" Jodie asked.

Laura shook her head. "No, he didn't mention any particulars. He just referred to his research and being persecuted by his professors. Kept talking about how he would get even with all of them."

"Where was he taking you? Did he say?" Fernando asked.

"To his house in the Cerrillos Hills. He said he would show me his laboratory. How's that for a pickup line?" Laura asked, flashing her ironic smile.

Jodie didn't laugh. She grabbed Laura's legs and helped her move them into the cruiser. "Let's get you to the ER."

"Nah, I'll be fine, I just need a warm bath," Laura said.

"No you won't," Jodie said, and climbed into the cruiser. Fernando followed.

Neither Fernando nor Laura argued with Jodie.

19

Fernando woke up with a headache. He was almost as tired as when he went to bed. They'd taken Laura to the Christus Saint Vincent Emergency Room last night, against her wishes. Fortunately Laura had no broken bones or other serious injuries, just bruises and lacerations. Even so, they spent a full three hours waiting around for one procedure or another, not to mention her discharge papers. By the time he made it home it was well past Midnight. Estelle was sound asleep when he crept like a thief into their bedroom.

He crawled out of bed and checked the clock on the nightstand: half past nine o'clock. No wonder he didn't see or hear Estelle this morning. He cleaned up as best he could and dressed in a clean set of clothes, jeans and a black Eddie Bauer shirt. Then he went to the kitchen and poured himself a cup of coffee, drank it quickly, and poured another. He never seemed to get enough coffee these days. The older he got, the more coffee he needed to wake up.

Sitting at the kitchen table, Fernando reflected on last night's events. They still didn't know the whereabouts of Anders' hideout, only that it was somewhere in the vicinity of Cerrillos, presumably in the hills behind Devil's Throne. They couldn't try to bait Anders again because he was on to their trap, so how would they ever find where he lived? That was a problem, a major problem. Not having any better ideas, he decided to return to Devil's Throne and look around in the daylight. He could search for the GPS Tracker Laura dropped and maybe some tire tracks near Devil's Throne that he could follow. First, though, he wanted to touch base with Jodie, so he called and left a message when she didn't answer.

In no great hurry to return to Cerrillos, Fernando spent some time sitting on his patio enjoying the blue sky and warm sun. He was thinking more and more about retiring completely from the profession, but first he wanted to bring Fidel's killer to justice. He owed his old friend that much. And he didn't want to let Dorothy down. For all these reasons he just couldn't quit the case now. He would make a decision when they finally caught Anders.

After a light lunch, Fernando headed out. He put his Smith & Wesson in the glove compartment of the Cherokee, just in case he needed it. Then he drove around the Paseo to Cerrillos Road and out to State Road 14. Everything looked more cheerful in the daylight than it did last night when they were following Anders. To the south Cedar Mountain and the Ortiz Mountains were crystal clear in the thin, dry air, their peaks towering in bas relief against the bright blue sky. His mind was a million miles away, remembering the times he'd hiked in the Ortiz when he was a young man and even when he and Estelle were first married. So preoccupied with his memories that he almost missed the turnoff to Cerrillos. Only the sight of the Galisteo Creek jolted him out of his memories and back to the moment.

Turning right, he drove into Cerrillos, noticing the line of cars parked near the Black Bird Saloon. A family of five, including three young boys, were climbing out of an old-fashioned station wagon as Fernando drove by the Cerrillos State Park Visitor Center. All five of them waved at him. He waved back. Then he turned onto the dirt road to Devil's Throne, retracing his route from the night before.

Approaching Devil's Throne, he saw two young men climbing the vertical front of the huge rock without ropes, using only their fingers and toes. Fernando pulled up beside their beat-up Volvo sedan and watched them climb for a few minutes. He didn't see how anyone could get any pleasure from climbing up a sheer rock, or bouldering as it was called, if he remembered correctly.

"Howdy," Fernando said, climbing out of his Cherokee

"Hey, pops," one of them replied, hanging by his fingers like a damn monkey. The other one ignored him.

After cursing under his breath at being called 'pops,' Fernando left the two climbers to their sport. He walked around behind the rock, where he'd searched the night before. He found the spot where the ground was torn up by Laura's struggle with Anders. There wasn't much to see, just dirt, sand, and a sprinkling of sage and chamisa bushes off to the side. He started there and walked in widening circles around the torn-up spot. He didn't find the GPS Tracker, but he did discover a set of tire tracks not far from the spot. There was no way to tell if the tracks were made by Anders' Toyota pickup, but they were in the correct location behind Devil's Throne. The tire tracks shot off into the desert, heading north by northwest. By the looks of the spewed sand all around and the ruts made by the tires, the vehicle must have squealed off quickly, the driver eager to get away.

Having no other leads, Fernando followed the tracks and hiked up to the top of a small rise. From the top of the rise he saw two tire tracks cutting across the mesa, over arroyos and around thick patches of chamisa and saltbush. Zig-zagging, but always headed northwest, until they disappeared into a series of round hills on the horizon. He decided to check it out.

Back at the Cherokee, Fernando buckled up for a rough ride. He drove off across the mesa, following the tracks as they snaked their way toward the distant hills. The path took him over a stretch of rocky terrain, followed by a sandy arroyo where his tires spun in the loose sand. He had to gun the big engine to get across the arroyo, skidding in the sand until the tires caught and he pitched forward over the far lip of the arroyo. From there the tire tracks veered left toward the first of the hills. He slowed down climbing the hill and stopped at the summit. To his left he saw a much-used dirt road heading west toward the small, unincorporated community of Waldo near Interstate 25. He ignored the road to Waldo. What interested him was the less-used spur that veered to the right into a canyon created by the surrounding hills.

The canyon, directly below him, stretched out to a sandstone cliff at its far end. In the canyon Fernando saw exactly what April had described: a small Ancestral Puebloan ruin built against the cliff, its red stone walls crumbling. Some of the stones had been used to build the foundation of a primitive cabin nearby. The cabin itself was constructed of rough-cut lumber with a couple of windows and a flat tin roof.

Even more troubling was a round, partly underground ruin on the floor of the canyon. With a stone foundation and black tar paper for a roof, the underground structure looked like the re-purposed ruins of a great kiva used by the Ancestral Puebloans for public ceremonies. He could tell by the two cardinal entrances, north and south, both with antechambers. Using a ruin like this would be a violation of the Antiquities Act and maybe the Native American Graves Protection and Repatriation Act. Serious business. But not as serious as murder.

Fernando didn't see any vehicles in the canyon. That meant he could have a look around undisturbed. He hoped. Instead of parking in the canyon, he drove around behind the hill where his Cherokee couldn't be seen. He debated whether to take his Smith & Wesson out of the glove compartment, but decided against it since he was only on a reconnaissance mission. Then he walked over the rise and into the canyon, heading for the south entrance to the underground structure. When he reached the entrance he stopped for a moment to look around, just to make sure there was no sign of Anders anywhere in the canyon.

Satisfied, he climbed down a series of earthen steps and into the semi-dark interior of what had been a great kiva. He knew for certain when he saw the interior features: a low masonry bench encircling the base of the room, a raised masonry firebox and deflector, four seating pits for roof supports, and raised floor vaults between the seating pits. A makeshift ceiling had been constructed with two-by-fours overlaid with thin sheets of paneling with tar paper on top. The underground structure had a close, earthy smell mixed with something else. Anders' herbs, he assumed.

After his eyes adjusted to the darkness, he moved past the firebox to a series of tables and shelves. One table had been converted into a bed, with hand and foot restraints attached on either side. On an adjoining table lay a pile of white sheets cut into strips of winding cloths. The shelves beyond contained multiple glass jars of herbs and powders, with an array of mixing bowls and pestles nearby, along with a small scale and other measuring instruments.

Fernando reached for one of the largest glass jars, which looked like the ones he'd seen in Galisteo at Gabe's herb shop.

Suddenly he heard a shuffling sound behind him.

Then a woman's voice: "Who are you? What are you doing here?"

20

Fernando froze and then turned slowly to find a tiny woman framed by sunlight coming in the southern entrance to the kiva. She seemed to have dark frizzy hair, but he couldn't make out any other features of her face because of the dim light. She held something in her hand that could have been a knife or a gun. That gave him pause. Fernando couldn't see her expression, but the tone of her voice suggested both anger and fear.

"Are you Melissa Vigil?" he asked, remembering Professor Satterfield telling him about the young woman who often accompanied Anders. His girlfriend maybe?

The woman ignored Fernando. "Who are you? What do you want?"

"I'm looking for Sven Anders. Name's Fernando Lopez."

"What do you want with him?" she asked. "Are you one of those people from the university?"

"No, I'm from Santa Fe," Fernando said. "I just wanted to ask him some questions."

"Yeah?" she asked, sounding skeptical. "They ruined his career. They tried to take away everything he's worked so hard for. They don't understand because he's a genius, he's not like them. He's doing the kind of research they're afraid to do. You have no idea—he's a true scientist. That's why they're afraid of him. They know he has the courage to do the important research that needs to be done. Otherwise their profession is a joke. A farce."

"Maybe so," Fernando replied, unable to hold his tongue, "but he also happens to be a murderer."

"Death is part of his research," she shot back. "Death and rebirth."

"What kind of research involves killing people and leaving their bodies around Cerrillos?" Fernando asked.

Again she ignored his question. "He'll be back shortly, and when he comes you better be gone if you know what's good for you. He doesn't allow anyone to come here...except me."

JAMES C. WILSON 99

Just then Fernando heard the sound of a vehicle coming into the canyon from the south. Probably up from the dirt road to Waldo. Probably Anders!

The young woman heard it too. She turned around and dashed out the southern entrance to the kiva. Moments later Fernando heard her calling for Andres outside. The vehicle stopped.

Unsure of what to do, Fernando moved to the northern entrance and waited. He heard a door slamming outside and then loud, excited voices. When he heard them approaching and then coming down the steps to the southern entrance, he sprinted out of the northern entrance and ran for the nearest hill, thinking it was where he'd parked his Cherokee. He scrambled up the side of the hill as fast as he could, slipping and sliding in the loose sand.

Looking over his shoulder he saw the tall, gangly Anders bounding up the hill after him. The much younger Anders kept gaining on him. Fernando struggled for breath.

Finally Anders caught Fernando from behind just as he reached the top of the hill. The two men went down together, hard. Anders jumped up first and kicked at Fernando, but Fernando grabbed Anders' foot and twisted it as hard as he could. Anders yelped in pain and fell backwards holding his leg.

Fernando seized his opportunity. He pounced on Anders, grabbing him by the neck and slamming him down into the ground repeatedly. Anders' head flopped from side to side, his wild shock of black hair covered with sand.

"So you like to kill women!" Fernando screamed, enraged. He dug his thumbs into Anders' windpipe, cutting off his oxygen. Anders' eyes rolled back in his head.

Fernando might have killed Anders, but suddenly a gunshot rang out behind him. He looked around and saw the young woman from the kiva climbing the hill and waving a pistol.

She fired again. This time sand kicked up just above him.

Fernando let go of Anders and scampered on all fours over the top of the hill as another shot rang out. Forgetting about Anders and the young woman, whoever she was, Fernando ran down the other side of the hill to his Cherokee and jumped into the driver's seat. The woman was just coming over the hill as he took off fast, skidding in the loose sand before his tires caught and he shot off toward Devil's Throne following the same tracks he'd followed earlier. He drove past Devil's Throne and took the dirt road into Cerrillos, stopping finally in front of the Black

Bird Saloon. Just in case Anders followed him, he wanted to be in a public place. With witnesses.

Fernando took his Smith & Wesson out of the glove department and waited, but Anders didn't appear. The trip had been a success. He'd done his job, finding Anders' hideout. Now it was up to Jodie and the authorities to bust Anders. After checking the rear view mirror one last time, Fernando took out his cell phone and called Jodie. Still no answer. She must have had some sort of emergency. So he left a message and asked her to call as soon as she could. Then he drove out of Cerrillos to State Road 14 and back to Santa Fe.

By the time he pulled into his office parking lot it was nearly three o'clock and Jodie hadn't called yet. He hurried into his office, not wanting to talk to anyone, especially the two tourists standing on the sidewalk looking at their map of Canyon Road. He didn't change the 'Closed' sign in his window. Instead, he went directly to his desk to check the blinking light on his answering machine. He found one message, not from Jodie but Hugh Satterfield. Surprised, Fernando punched the replay button and listened to the message:

"Mister Lopez, Hugh Satterfield from UNM here. We talked the other day about Sven Anders and you left your card in case I had any other information about Sven. Well, I thought you should know that I just received a strange, threatening letter from him. It came in the mail this morning. It reads: 'Satterfield, by the power of three, so mote it be, watch your back, beware what you see.'"

Fernando interrupted Satterfield. "The power of three? What the hell does that mean?"

"It's an old witch's curse, supposed to have magical powers," Satterfield explained. "I'd like to think this is just the musings of a disgruntled student, but I know Anders and he's, well...not your ordinary student. He's older, more resourceful, more dangerous. Given his obsession with the dark arts, he's literally capable of just about anything. So I'm calling to ask your advice. Should I inform the police about this matter? I hate to involve the police because of all the negative feedback we received after expelling Anders. Let's just say the provost is not a happy camper, but on the other hand Anders, by his own testimony, is quite capable of doing great harm. I would very much appreciate it if you returned my call and advised me."

Fernando didn't know what to make of Satterfield's day of the witch scenario, but he called the professor back out of a sense of duty.

"Satterfield here," the professor answered.

"Fernando Lopez returning your call," Fernando said. "I got

your message, and I can understand your concern. I usually tell people in your situation to contact the police, if only to make them aware of the situation. I just had a violent confrontation with Anders out at his place near Cerrillos. You know him better than I do, but based on what I experienced I would say yes, call the police. Maybe the Albuquerque Police have this guy on their radar, who knows?"

"What happened between you and Anders?" Satterfield asked.

"I discovered where Anders has been staying," Fernando said. "He's converted an Ancestral Puebloan ruin near Cerrillos into his laboratory, as he calls it."

"What kind of ruin?" Satterfield asked.

"An underground dwelling, looks like it was once a Great Kiva," Fernando responded.

Satterfield sputtered. "Oh my God, he doesn't know what he's doing. Or if he does, the man is absolutely mad. He's in violation of the Antiquities Act and in danger of bringing down whatever bad juju he claims to believe in on himself. He's a damned fool!"

Fernando went on to describe what he had seen at Anders' laboratory. Then he recounted his violent encounters with the young woman in the kiva and then with Anders on the hill.

"That's his accomplice, Melissa Vigil," Satterfield said. "She follows him everywhere."

"So I gathered," Fernando said.

"What's deeply troubling is that Sven is actually going through with his immersion research idea, where he performs these ritual acts in violation of every codification of science ethics and civil law since the Age of Reason. We don't believe in witches anymore, and for good reason. They don't exist!"

Fernando sighed. "Well, apparently Anders does believe in witches, or at least something like witches. The idea that his herbs and potions can end and then restart life. Something like that."

"Nonsense," Satterfield muttered.

"But going back to your question, I would contact the police," Fernando said. "Then if Anders does come after you, they'll be aware of the situation."

Satterfield did not respond.

After a few seconds Fernando asked, "Are you still there?"

"Yes...thank you," Satterfield said and clicked off.

Fernando placed his cell phone on the desk. He sat in his chair brooding, waiting for a call from Jodie. None came.

21

By the time Jodie finally called next morning Fernando was in his study researching Sven Anders. He wanted to find out what Satterfield had meant when he said they'd received 'negative feedback' after expelling Anders. Negative feedback from whom? When he Googled Anders he found one news article in the *Albuquerque Enquirer*. The story quoted Anders as saying that expelling him demonstrated the "Eurocentric, racist mindset of the Anthropology Department and the university in general." Supporting Anders were several Native American and Hispanic groups, as well as one prominent folklore society, all of which criticized the university for their short-sided, anti-intellectual blindness and unwillingness to explore what they didn't understand, namely Native folklore, mythology, and history. In response, the university defended its action as based on hard science, which rang hollow, given the preponderance of critics quoted in the article.

As one of Anders' supporters said, "One person's science is another person's witchcraft."

Jodie's call brought Fernando back to the present. He closed his computer screen and picked up his cell phone. "Jodie, I've been trying to get in touch with you."

"Yeah, sorry...we had a five-vehicle accident on La Bajada Hill yesterday, semi trucks and all," Jodie said. "Took us all day to clean up the mess. Several injuries, but luckily no deaths. So what's up?"

"Big news. I located Anders," Fernando said. "He's staying in a shack on a dirt road behind Devil's Throne. I saw the pit-house April mentioned, an old kiva that Anders partially restored. He apparently conducts his so-called research there. I didn't get a chance to investigate, because Anders and his companion, Melissa Vigil, surprised me. The three of us tangled, but I managed to get away. I can take you right to it, whenever you're ready."

"I'm ready," Jodie said. "I can pick you up at your office. How soon can you be there?"

"Give me ten minutes," Fernando said.

"Okay, see you in ten. You can tell me about what you saw on our way down to Cerrillos," Jodie said, clicking off.

Fernando grabbed his Smith & Wesson and locked the house on his way out. He thought he would have time to check his messages in his office before Jodie arrived, but by the time he drove around the Paseo to Canyon Road and up to his office he found Jodie's cruiser in his parking lot. He pulled in beside the cruiser and jumped out of his Cherokee.

Jodie lowered her driver's side window and said, "Let's roll."

Fernando climbed into her cruiser as Jodie took off down Canyon Road. "Jesus, you could at least wait until I'm in the car and buckled up," Fernando said, irritated.

Jodie glanced at him "You are in the car."

They raced around the Paseo to Cerrillos Road and out to State Road 14. Fernando relaxed a little when they got out of city traffic. Jodie drove fast, her eyes fixed on the highway ahead.

"So what did you see in the pit-house?" Jodie asked. "You said you didn't have time to investigate, but you must have seen something if they went after you."

"Like I said, he's using the ruin of a Great Kiva for his experiments," Fernando said. "He built a roof over the ruin out of particle board and tar paper. I saw a long table with restraints where he bound his victims and shelves stacked with bottles of herbs and chemicals, whatever he's using on the people he abducts. That's about all I saw. It was pitch dark and I didn't have much time to look around before Anders and Vigil surprised me."

"No lab notes or records?" Jodie asked. "What about a computer. Did you see a computer anywhere?"

Fernando shook his head. "No, I didn't see a computer. In fact, there was no electricity in the pit-house."

"Well, Anders probably uses a laptop," Jodie replied. "He could charge it at any nearby Starbucks—any restaurant or public facility."

At the Cerrillos intersection, Jodie turned right and drove into town past the Black Bird Saloon. She slowed down, waiting for directions to the pit-house. "How do I get there?"

"Straight ahead," Fernando said. "Take Waldo Canyon Road west. The dirt road to the pit-house will be off to the right. Heading north."

Jodie followed his directions.

As soon as they cleared Cerrillos they saw the smoke. Large, billowing clouds of black smoke rose over the mesa to the northwest. The black clouds slowly dissipated as they floated skyward. Jodie pointed at the smoke. "Don't tell me that's where we're going?"

"Looks like it," Fernando said, beginning to worry. Now what?

Jodie turned off on a dirt road that curved toward the smoke. As they approached the acrid smell of the fire stung their nostrils. Over the last rise Jodie stopped the cruiser. Below them they saw a scene of devastation. The entire pit-house was an inferno, its roof having collapsed into the flames. From a distance it looked like a huge bonfire someone had started for some kind of celebration, except the smoke was as black as charcoal. In contrast, the stone house against the cliff only smoldered, its stones blackened and its door and windows blown out by the force of a fire inside.

A red rescue pumper belonging to the Galisteo Volunteer Fire Department was parked at the end of the road, near the kiva. Three firefighters worked to extinguish the blaze, two men holding the fire-hose and another spraying foam around the edges of the northern entrance to the kiva. As water in the pumper started to run low the flames finally began to die down. Eventually the below-ground structure became a black hole of smoldering mush with pockets of flames licking the few small objects that remained discernible.

Fernando and Jodie watched from the rise, not wanting to get in the way of the firefighters. When the water stopped, Jodie waved and walked down the hill to identify herself. Fernando stayed back, walking instead to the lip of the kiva. Nothing remained but black mush, a mixture of water and ash. The roof supports, the tables, the shelves, the glass jars, everything had disintegrated in the fire. A fire that intense had to have been started on purpose, with an accelerant.

While Jody talked to the Galisteo volunteers, Fernando walked to the burnt-out stone house against the cliff. Still smoldering, the inside of the house remained too hot to enter. From the gap where the door had been he saw the same blackened mush he'd seen at the kiva. He looked carefully for any sign of human remains but found no trace. Same as the kiva. Looked to him like Anders and maybe Melissa Vigil had torched the place and fled.

Satisfied, Fernando joined Jodie talking to the firefighters. Jodie introduced Fernando and said, "The fire was reported by a couple of climbers at Devil's Throne this morning."

"About eight o'clock," the oldest of the three firefighters said. He seemed to be their leader, a heavyset man wearing jeans and a Nike sweatshirt. "When we got here the place was already lost. Noting much we could do except put out the flames. Keep it from spreading to the grasses on the hillside."

Jodie nodded. "And you think the fire was intentionally started."

"Definitely," the man said. "There's nothing here that would start a fire, no electricity or natural gas. Plus Dick over there smelled gasoline when we arrived. Down by the entrance there." He pointed to the southern entrance.

"More like diesel fuel," Dick said. "A strong odor of diesel fuel."

"Do you know anything about this Sven Anders who was living here?" Jodie asked.

The older guy shook his head. "Never heard of him. We don't come over here very often. Mostly stay in the Galisteo area."

Dick stepped up. "These are Pueblo ruins. Whoever did this is facing some serious jail time under the Antiquities Act. Crazy sonofabitch. Why would he set fire to a kiva?"

"Bad Karma, for sure," the youngest of the three firefighters said, a short stocky man with ear-rings and tattoos on both arms.

"Yeah, well, Anders has worse problems than the Antiquities Act," Jodie said.

The firefighters glanced at Jodie, who didn't explain.

Yes he does, Fernando thought. Wherever he was.

22

Jodie pulled off the dirt road and parked behind Devil's Throne. She killed the engine and climbed out of the cruiser. Leaning against the back of the huge rock, she folded her arms across her chest and stared at Fernando, who sat in the passenger's seat not knowing what she wanted. Finally he climbed out of the cruiser and joined her leaning against the rock.

"Clearly they've run," Jodie said. "They tried their best to destroy all the evidence in the two structures and then bolted. All I can do at this point is put out an APB on the red Toyota pickup. You said it was a Tundra, right? I'll get the license from motor vehicles and put out the APB as soon as I get back to my office. I know you want to apprehend Anders because he killed your friend, but once he's out of Santa Fe County, my options are limited. As you know."

Fernando nodded. "Understood."

"Do you have any other ideas?" Jodie asked.

"Well, I didn't tell you, but right before you called this morning I talked to Professor Satterfield, the Chair of the Anthropology Department at the University of New Mexico. He told me the department received a lot of bad publicity when they kicked out Anders for his dark obsessions with witchcraft and cannibalism. He also said he'd just received a threatening letter in the mail from Anders, which he read as a death threat. So Anders may be headed for Albuquerque now, preparing to attack Satterfield. I suppose I could check out his former residence in Albuquerque, the house where I saw him earlier, taking some of his belongings out of the garage. That's where he hit me over the head with a chair."

"Yeah, that's Bernalillo County, so you would have to do it by yourself or with the Albuquerque Police," Jodie said. "Did Satterfield tell the Police about his death threat?"

Fernando shook his head. "I don't know. I told him to report it to the police, but I don't know if he followed through."

With that, they climbed into the cruiser and drove back to Santa Fe. When Jodie dropped him off at his office on Canyon Road, she said, "Keep me informed, okay? I'll do the same if anything pops up."

Fernando walked down the gravel path to his office. He hadn't spent much time in his office lately, so he placed his 'Open' sign in the front window and opened wide the side windows. He needed the fresh air. Noticing the blinking light on his desk phone, he sat at the desk and pushed the replay button. When he saw the message was from Dorothy Rodriguez, he felt the usual wave of remorse and guilt sweep over him. He knew he should have contacted her earlier, even if Fidel's killer was still on the loose. He listened:

"Hi Fernando, it's Dorothy. I'm calling to ask if you've made any progress in finding Fidel's killer. I haven't heard from you in a while and I just…well, I just wanted to know. We missed you at Fidel's memorial. It was lovely to see all his old friends and to know so many people loved him. I still can't believe he's really gone, we were together so long, you know…."

Fernando felt bad. Fidel had been one of his oldest friends. Dorothy too. He bit the bullet and called Dorothy back. She answered immediately.

"Dorothy, hi," Fernando said. "I'm so sorry I haven't gotten back to you earlier. I was out of town for Fidel's memorial. I feel terrible about missing that. I want you to know I was there in spirit."

"Well, we missed you too," Dorothy responded.

"I do have some news," Fernando said. "We found the guy who killed Fidel and the other woman. He was living outside Cerrillos in a primitive house—Sven Anders is his name. Before the sheriff could arrest him, he set fire to his house and took off. We're looking for him now."

"So you haven't caught him, then…." Dorothy said weakly, a hint of weariness in her voice.

"No, but we expect to soon," Fernando added, but Dorothy did not respond. Instead, she hung up her phone.

Now Fernando really felt like a bastard. Not only had he missed Fidel's memorial, he'd basically lied to Dorothy. He'd chosen not to attend the memorial because he just couldn't face it—the service, the old friends, the loss of Fidel.

Depressed, Fernando found himself going to the dark place. He needed to take a break, get away from his work and his routine. Do something different.

Then it occurred to him, a stroke of genius. One of his favorite things to do when he was younger was to hike the Windsor Trail to Santa

Fe Baldy. He and his friends would often meet at the Santa Fe Ski Basin early Saturday morning and spend the day hiking to Baldy and back, a thirteen or fourteen mile hike. They would take water, sometimes beer, and spend the day on the mountain. The last time he hiked the trail was with Fidel and Antonio, so it seemed only appropriate now that he would hike the trail for Fidel, as a kind of penance for missing his memorial. He wondered if he should call Antonio, but realized Antonio would be at work at this hour. So he decided to go by himself.

Fernando took his backpack out of the closet and grabbed a couple bottles of water from his mini-fridge. Then he closed his windows and locked up. Without calling Estelle or letting anyone know where he was going, he climbed into his Cherokee and drove down to the Paseo and around to Hyde Park Road, the way to the Ski Basin. He followed the twisting highway into the national forest, the huge ponderosa pines and then the aspens as he climbed higher in elevation. The forest seemed to close in around him, taking away his troubles. Nothing but a vision of green trees and blue sky, as timeless as it was serene. He noticed some of the aspen leaves had begun to take on a yellowish hue, foretelling the chilly fall weather coming soon. The forest and the mountains had always been healing for him, no more so than today. For the first time in weeks he felt free, light as bird. And content.

When he came to the ski basin, he steered to the northwest corner of the parking lot. Two other vehicles were parked near the trailhead. He hoisted his backpack and locked the Cherokee. Then he started up the first hill to the trailhead. He didn't need to look at the signs or a map, he knew the trail by heart. As he cleared the first meadow and started down the narrow trail that circumvented Lake Peak he saw two young women coming toward him. They both wore cut-off jean shorts and western hats, chatting and laughing nonstop.

Fernando waved and said, "Howdy, ladies."

The two women giggled and said hello.

Then he walked off by himself into a wall of green. Visibility on this part of the trail was limited, so he looked up at the mountain on his right, which seemed to touch the sky. Breathing the clean mountain air, he moved slowly, rhythmically down the trail, one foot after another, losing all sense of time. Eventually the trail turned right as it circled the mountain. From that point on he had a clear view of the massive Santa Fe Baldy to the north, across a deep valley. He stopped for a moment to appreciate the rocky summit of Baldy, some 12,600 feet above sea level. Someone had piled stones on the summit, like a beacon attracting hikers from the several trails that converged on Baldy from all directions.

Fernando started to tire as he approached the Rio Nambe, the halfway point of the trek to the top of Baldy. From there the trail swung north and proceeded up the side of Baldy. He sat down to rest beside the Rio Nambe, which at this time of year was just a trickle of water flowing down from the mountain. He took off his backpack and opened one of the bottles of water. He had no idea of the time and didn't particularly care, but he saw the sun already sinking in the western sky. He wouldn't have time to reach the summit. Maybe he would come back another day with Antonio, soon. Leaning against a boulder, he watched a bank of thin white clouds float over the top of Baldy. Just watched the clouds.

This spot, he remembered, was where he and Fidel and Antonio typically stopped to rest before their final ascent. Last time he recalled Fidel passing around a flask of brandy or cognac, one of those spirits. Then Antonio had passed around a joint. By the time they resumed their hike they were feeling no pain. And they made it to the top, as they did every single time they came.

Good times. Good memories.

At peace with the universe, Fernando grabbed his pack and headed back to the ski basin.

23

This morning Fernando had a plan. He felt refreshed by yesterday's hike in the mountains. The exercise and fresh air had cleared his head. He realized last night that one way to find Anders would be to locate Melissa Vigil, the young woman who seemed to be Anders' companion. Since she, like Anders, had been a UNM Anthropology student and had been coming to classes with Anders, he decided to call the secretary in the Anthropology Department. She'd given him Anders' last known address; maybe she could do the same for Melissa Vigil.

So after breakfast he took his cell phone and his third cup of coffee into his study and dialed the UNM Anthropology Department. The phone rang several times and then a recorded message played: "Hello, you have reached the University of New Mexico's Anthropology Department. The department is currently closed indefinitely due to an emergency. You may leave a message, but no one is currently available to return your call. Thank you."

Puzzled, Fernando decided to call Professor Satterfield. Maybe Satterfield would know how to find Melissa Vigil's address. He browsed his recent calls on his cell phone and clicked on Satterfield's number.

"Mister Lopez, you must be psychic," Satterfield answered.

"What do you mean?" Fernando asked.

"Oh, I thought you'd heard about the poisoning," Satterfield said.

Confused, Fernando asked, "Poisoning? You've been poisoned?"

"No, sorry, let me explain," Satterfield said. "Someone attacked the department office with ricin. The person responsible pried open the office door and tossed in a glass jar filled with powdered ricin. The jar exploded on the floor and spread the powder everywhere—on the floor, on the furniture, and in the air. The office is considered off limits, the site of a police action at the moment. We won't be able to use the office until a team from the Los Alamos Lab comes to clean it up next week. I can hardly believe this happened at UNM. Ricin?"

"Well, it's not as uncommon as you think," Fernando said. "Ricin is easy to make. You can find recipes all over the internet. All you need are castor beans, which are easy to get. They grow wild around here. You turn the beans into mush, squeeze out the oil, and dry what's left until you can grind it to fine powder. The fine powder is lethal, especially if it gets into your lungs."

"Hmmm...." Satterfield said.

"You think Anders could have done this?" Fernando asked.

"I dunno. He certainly has the expertise," Satterfield replied. "And he did send me a threatening letter."

"That's basically why I'm calling," Fernando said. "We found Anders, but before we could bring him in for questioning he torched the place and took off. The last time we saw him, he was with Melissa Vigil. So we wondered if you knew, or knew how to find, Melissa Vigil's address. I first called the office, thinking your secretary could provide the address. That's when I found the message on the department extension and called you instead."

Satterfield sighed. "Yes, poor Shirley. She was the first to arrive at the office yesterday morning and to find the powder. Unfortunately, she inhaled enough to make her very sick while waiting for the police. She's in the hospital now. Her doctors wanted to intubate her last night but she resisted. Thank God she's better this morning. I just now left UNM Hospital."

"Sorry to hear that," Fernando said.

"Anyway, Melissa Vigil's address, let's see," Satterfield said, mostly to himself. "Thing is, the registrar wouldn't give you that information because of the privacy issue I mentioned earlier. But we do require the people who visit or audit our classes to fill out forms, just so we have some record of who's there, in case a problem arises. I believe Shirley gave me the forms at the beginning of the semester. If so, they're in the top drawer of my desk at school."

"But isn't the office closed?"

"The department office, yes," Satterfield replied. "But my personal office is at the end of the hall. The ricin powder did get into the air filtration system, but insofar as I know it's only been detected in the adjoining offices. Apparently. I say apparently because I don't think the police know for sure."

"So there is some risk," Fernando said.

"Yes, but if it will help you find Anders and Melissa Vigil, I'm willing to meet you there," Satterfield said. "We could wear masks, like we did for Covid."

"Okay, can you meet this afternoon?" Fernando asked. "Say one o'clock?"

"Of course. I'll meet you in front of our building," Satterfield said, clicking off quickly.

Not happy about this latest course of events, Fernando sat at his desk brooding. That's all he needed, fucking ricin. The fact that Anders was able and willing to use ricin to get revenge frightened him. A weapon of international terrorists, ricin wasn't as easy to manufacture as he had led Satterfield to believe. It took knowledge and the right tools to produce ricin from castor beans. If Anders could do this, that meant he was incredibly dangerous. Much more dangerous than Fernando thought. All of which meant they had to find and stop him fast. Damned fast.

Melissa Vigil might be the key. If they could find Melissa, it was possible that she would lead them to Anders. A big if, Fernando knew. But what else did they have to work with? Nada!

24

Fernando arrived at the University of New Mexico a few minutes before one o'clock. As before, he parked in the Maxwell Museum parking lot. He paid the meter and walked around the Maxwell to the Anthropology Building, where he found Professor Satterfield waiting for him outside the front door. The tall, stout man with the shock of gray hair waved. Fernando noticed Satterfield wore a navy blazer over jeans today, not a suit.

Satterfield pointed to the barricade and yellow caution tape blocking the front door. "We had to move our offices to a temporary location, but I can still get in my office here. Did you bring a mask?" he asked, taking an N95 mask out of his breast pocket.

"I did," Fernando said, taking his N95 out of his shirt pocket. He had no idea if an N95 worked with ricin, but he figured it was better than nothing.

"Follow me," Satterfield said.

Masked, Fernando followed Satterfield around the barricade and into the front entrance. The professor's personal office was at the end of the long hallway. On the way they passed the department office, sealed tight with warning signs posted on the door and the surrounding walls. Looked abandoned and a bit forlorn. No one else was in the hallway or, as far as they could tell, the building.

Satterfield unlocked his office door and stepped inside.

Fernando followed cautiously, looking around for white powder that had settled on the furniture or the floor. He saw none.

Meanwhile, Satterfield sat at his desk and opened the top drawer. He looked through the drawer and then mumbled something under his breath, slamming the drawer closed. Then he opened one of the side drawers and rifled through his files. This time he found what he was looking for, a manila folder holding an assortment of letterhead and legal pad sheets. He held up one of the yellow sheets and said, "Here it is, Melissa Vigil's address. Let me write it down for you."

Fernando waited while Satterfield copied the address and then handed him the paper.

"Thanks," Fernando said, glancing at the address on South 6th Street. "Where is this?"

Satterfield glanced at him. "Well, it's in the old Barelas neighborhood. Not far from the National Hispanic Cultural Center on Fourth Street, if you know where that is. Just a couple of blocks over and not quite as far south."

Fernando nodded. He'd visited the National Hispanic Cultural Center several times and knew the area well enough to get around.

"Okay," Satterfield said, looking around. "Let's get the hell out of here before someone finds us."

Fernando followed Satterfield outside and removed his mask. "Thanks."

"No problem," Satterfield said. "Keep in touch. Please let me know if you find Anders. I'll breath a lot easier when you apprehend him. What about Vigil? Will she be arrested too?"

"Good question," Fernando said, shaking his head. "That depends on what the sheriff decides to do. Which will depend on her role in all this, whether she's an accessory or what. She fired a couple of shots in my direction back in Cerrillos when Anders and I were wrestling, but I think that might have been just to break up the fight. So I don't know the extent of her involvement."

"Yes, I understand," Satterfield said. "She never said much when she showed up in class with Anders. Very passive, that's how I would describe her."

"Okay, I'll keep you posted at my end, you do the same," Fernando said.

With that, Fernando walked back to the parking lot by the Maxwell Museum. He climbed into his Cherokee and drove down University Boulevard to Central Avenue, the historic Route 66. On Central he headed west, entering downtown Albuquerque. When he passed Hotel Andaluz he knew he was close to 6th Street. Four blocks later he turned left and proceeded slowly down 6th Street, looking for the address Satterfield had given him. When he saw it, he pulled over to the curb and studied the house, a large tan-colored adobe with a carport in the driveway instead of a garage. A bank of colorful red and purple hollyhocks gave the adobe a festive look, as did the front door and window frames, all painted a bright blue color. Clearly, Melissa Vigil came from a middle class family.

Fernando stepped out of the Cherokee and walked up the sidewalk to the house. A dog barked next door, alerting the sleepy neighborhood that a stranger had arrived. On the porch he rang the doorbell and then knocked lightly on the door. When it opened, a short plump woman with shoulder-length gray hair stood in the doorway. She looked to be in her mid to late fifties, but she had a friendly smile that gave her a youthful look. Pleasant.

"Hi, can I help you?" she asked.

"I'm looking for Melissa Vigil," Fernando said. "I was given this address by the Chairman of the Anthropology Department at UNM."

Suddenly a shadow fell across the woman's face. Not pronounced, but clearly visible. As if the mention of Melissa had darkened her day.

"I see," she said, but offered nothing more.

"I'm sorry," Fernando said, trying to ease the situation. "My name is Fernando Lopez, I'm a private investigator. Are you Melissa's mom?"

The woman nodded. "Yes, I'm Kate Vigil. Why are you looking for Melissa?"

"Well, actually, I'm looking for Sven Anders," Fernando said. "He was last seen with Melissa. I thought she might know where he is."

Kate sighed. "Come in."

Fernando followed her into the front living room. She motioned for him to sit on a burgundy colored sofa, while she took a seat in a matching Queen Anne chair. The walls of the room sparkled with bright paintings and photographs, thanks to the sunshine flooding the room through a bank of windows overlooking 6th Street. The light and bright colors made the interior of the house as cheerful as the exterior.

"Melissa is a lost child," Kate said. "She only occasionally comes home. Mostly she stays with friends. Partly that's because she doesn't get along with her stepfather. He works for the city and doesn't approve of her freewheeling lifestyle. Nor do I, for that matter."

"How did she get hooked up with Anders?" Fernando asked.

Kate shook her head. "She went back to school last year as an anthropology major and met Sven Anders in one of her classes. I think he was some sort of graduate assistant. Anyway, she fell under his spell. We think they're having relations. Thank God she's on birth control pills."

"Has Melissa mentioned that Anders was expelled from UNM?"

"No, but I'm not surprised," Kate said. "Anders is very strange. Strange and frightening, in fact. Always talking about spells and curses, stuff like that. Gives me the creeps."

Fernando nodded. "Do you know who Melissa has been staying with, when she's not here?"

"No, she doesn't tell us much. She's an adult, with her own life. What can you do?" Kate asked, opening her arms wide.

"Yeah, what can you do," Fernando repeated. "My wife and I went through the same thing with our oldest daughter, who had a mind of her own. Very strong-willed. Used to drive my wife crazy."

"Then you know what it's like," Kate said. "But if you really want to talk to Melissa, you might try her workplace. She works evenings, five P.M. to closing on Tuesday through Saturday, as a waitress at a restaurant called County Line on Tramway. It's way out on Tramway near the mountains. Almost on the Sandia Indian Reservation."

"Thanks, I might do that," Fernando said. "We think Anders is very dangerous. He's the chief suspect in two separate murders. It would be good for Melissa if you could get her to stay away from him."

"We're trying, believe me," Kate said, shaking her head. "Two murders? Oh my God!"

Fernando did believe her. She seemed genuine. He thanked her again and left.

Outside, he sat in his Cherokee for a few minutes thinking. He hated driving back and forth to Albuquerque, so why not show up at County Line about five o'clock this afternoon? He could confront Melissa and then head back to Santa Fe. He figured he could make it back by six thirty.

He had a plan.

25

Since he had over two hours to kill before Melissa reported for work, Fernando decided to return to UNM and go for a walk around the campus. He still had fond memories of the two years he'd spent at UNM before family responsibilities forced him to leave school and get a job. He drove back to Central Avenue and up to the campus and then parked in the Maxwell Museum lot. Taking his time, he strolled past the duck pond and Zimmerman Library. At the Student Union he finally stopped and took a seat on one of the benches out front.

Watching the students walk by made him smile. Everyone looked so young, especially the coeds, most of whom still wore shorts and skimpy shirts. Hard to imagine being that young. Lost in thought, he wondered if he would change anything if he could go back in time and live his life again. Probably not. Mostly he'd been driven by need, not choice. He'd always done what he had to do, even if like everyone else he wanted to believe in free will. Maybe in the end they were all buffeted by necessity or fate, whatever you wanted to call it.

Finally Fernando came to his senses and checked the time. Nearly four o'clock. He figured it would take him at least half an hour to drive to the County Line restaurant, so he left the bench and walked back to his Cherokee. He didn't know Albuquerque all that well, but he was familiar with the major thoroughfares. Tramway was the major north-south boulevard at the eastern edge of the city, running along the Sandia Mountains. To get there he followed I-25 North to Paseo del Norte, which took him East across town to Tramway. Turning left, he headed north toward the Sandia Indian Reservation. Here the highway kissed the foothills of the Sandias, triangular shaped green hills that rose like steps to the top of Sandia Mountain, nearly eleven thousand feet above sea level.

Up ahead Fernando saw County Line off to the right, just before Tramway swung to the left and abutted the reservation. A sprawling, garish building with a row of large windows in front and a blue neon sign overhead, the restaurant looked like a country road house and honky-tonk. He turned into the nearly empty parking lot that wrapped around the front and far side of the building and then parked across from the front entrance. He backed the Cherokee into the parking space so that he would be facing anyone who entered the restaurant.

A few minutes before five p.m. the restaurant employees began arriving. They parked off to the side of the building and walked across the parking lot to the front entrance. Most of the employees looked much older than Melissa, but then he saw a blue Honda Civic driven by a young woman. He waited, and sure enough a tiny woman with frizzy black hair stepped out of the Civic and began walking toward the front entrance. She wore black tights and a flannel shirt and walked in short, jerky steps. It was Melissa Vigil.

Fernando climbed out of the Cherokee and walked diagonally across the parking lot to cut her off as she approached the entrance. He couldn't help but notice how incredibly young she looked in the soft afternoon light.

She stopped when she saw him approaching. "Oh God, not you! What do you want?"

"I want to know where your friend Sven Anders is," Fernando said. "He's a murderer and has to be stopped."

"How would I know," she shot back. "He dropped me off at my parents' house after he was stupid enough to burn down his house and lab. He only comes by when he wants to screw me anyway."

Fernando smiled. She did remind him of Flavia, his oldest daughter, who was just as high-spirited in her younger days. Just as feisty. "His lab? You mean the ancestral kiva that he trashed in violation of the Antiquities Act?"

"Whatever," she snapped and turned to walk away.

Fernando grabbed her arm and spun her around. Then he grabbed her by the shoulders and said, "Listen, Melissa, you almost killed me the day before yesterday when you fired those shots. I haven't reported the shooting yet, but unless you change your attitude and start cooperating, I'll go to the sheriff and file a criminal complaint. You understand?"

She stared at him, tongue-tied. Finally she spoke. "I'm telling you the truth. I don't know where he went after he dropped me off. I'm sorry, but I have to report for work now."

Fernando didn't believe her. If Anders had dropped her off at her parents' house, her mother would have mentioned it to him. Kate hated Anders and would do anything to keep her daughter away from him.

"Here," Fernando said, giving her one of his cards.

Just then a pickup pulled into the parking lot across the way. A redneck cowboy type stumbled out of the van, an empty Budweiser can clanging on the pavement behind him. The cowboy swayed over to them and said, "Hey fella, leave the little girl alone."

Neither Fernando nor Melissa responded.

"You hear me or what," the cowboy said and shoved Fernando.

Fernando frowned. "Mind your own business, friend."

But the cowboy shoved Fernando again. Big mistake.

Fernando crouched and drove his right hand, propelled by 185 pounds of lean muscle, into the cowboy's gut. The cowboy yelped and sank to his knees, gasping for breath.

Melissa shook her head at both of them, Fernando and the cowboy. "I have to start work," she said, turning away. She headed for the front entrance.

"I'll be in touch," Fernando called after her.

Melissa turned and gave him the finger.

Fernando had to laugh. Yeah, just like Flavia. Then he heard the cowboy stirring on the pavement behind him.

"Whoa...did you get the number of that truck?" the cowboy said, crawling on all fours now.

"Here, let me help you up," Fernando said. He extended a hand and helped the cowboy upright. The young man brushed himself off and mumbled something.

"You better get something to eat and some coffee," Fernando said, patting the cowboy on the back. Fernando turned him facing the stairway up to the restaurant and then gave him a nudge forward.

Swaying, the cowboy managed to make it up the steps one at a time and into County Line.

As soon as the cowboy was safely inside the restaurant, Fernando climbed into his Cherokee and headed for Santa Fe.

26

Fernando was sound asleep when Estelle woke him next morning. He could tell she still had a burr in her saddle by how hard she shook him. Last night he'd made the mistake of not calling to tell her he would be home late, as per their agreement. Somewhere along the line he'd lost track of time. After leaving the County Line parking lot, he'd taken his time driving back to Santa Fe and then stopped off at El Farol for a Modelo with Ruby and the Canyon Road gang, trying to relax. By the time he'd made it home it was half past seven.

"Wake up, Jodie's called several times on your cell phone," she said.

He grumbled something and sat up in bed. "Okay."

Pausing a moment to get his wits about him, Fernando climbed out of bed and checked the time. Eight o'clock exactly. By the time he pulled on a pair of jeans and hobbled bare-foot to the kitchen Estelle had already left for work. He heard her Camry drive off down Acequia Madre toward the Paseo. He poured himself a cup of coffee from the pot Estelle had left him and looked for his cell phone, which he found on the kitchen counter.

After a few sips of coffee, he sat down at the kitchen table with his cell phone and clicked on Jodie's number.

"Hey, Fernando, I have some news," she answered.

"Yeah, me too," he said. "You first."

"You won't believe this," Jodie said. "We got the final toxicology report on the first mummy woman we found in Cerrillos. She had ricin in her system as well as Wolfsbane. Ricin!"

When Fernando didn't respond, Jodie said, "You don't seem surprised."

"I'm not," Fernando said, and told her about Satterfield and what had happened at the UNM Anthropology Department. "So apparently Anders has been using ricin as one of his poisons all along."

"Apparently," Jodie said. "But that's not all. We got a call yesterday afternoon from a couple of hikers who climbed Devil's Throne. They decided to pitch camp behind it on the mesa there and spend the night. When they started setting up, they found two shallow graves. They called us right away, and we went out with forensics. We found two more women wrapped in white sheets like mummies, one fairly recent. Forensics thought the other one was at least a year old, given how the body was decomposed. So it looks like Anders has been killing women for at least a year. I'm on my way back to Devil's Throne now and thought you might want to join us."

"Okay, I'll meet you there," Fernando said, shaking his head, and clicked off.

Just what he needed to start the day: more dead bodies. Between the proliferation of mummies in Cerrillos and the ricin attack in Albuquerque, he had his hands full. And he was supposed to be retired.

Grumbling, Fernando gobbled some cold cereal for breakfast and then dressed quickly. He didn't know which was worse—decomposing mummies or ricin. Looked like today he would have to deal with decomposing mummies.

Though up and about, he didn't actually leave the house until after nine o'clock. He took his time again this morning, because he was damn tired of driving to Cerrillos and in no great hurry to revisit Devil's Throne. By the time he turned off Cerrillos Road onto State Road 14, he regretted not stopping at a Starbucks for more coffee. He'd left the house without drinking his usual three cups. Big mistake.

Fernando drove through Cerrillos, spotting the cruiser as soon as he turned onto the dirt road to Devil's Throne. Jodie and two men stood in a saddleback between two hills behind Devil's Throne. Probably the two hikers who'd found the graves.

When she saw Fernando, Jodie motioned for him to join them. He climbed out of the Cherokee and made his way across the dirt road to a gradual incline leading up to where the three of them stood talking. Behind them a length of yellow caution tape roped off the hillside.

As he walked Fernando noticed the ground was sandy here, not solid rock like Devil's Throne itself. It would be relatively easy to dig a quick, shallow grave to get rid of a dead body. The rises on either side of the saddleback were gradual, of no interest to hikers, which explained why the graves hadn't been found sooner. No reason for a climber to come up here.

Jodie stood head to head with the two hikers, just as tall and as muscular as the two young men dressed in hiking clothes. Both wore long-sleeve sun shirts, polyester pants that converted to shorts by means of zippered pant legs, and climbing shoes. And both wore sunhats over their youthful, sunburned faces. They looked cheerful, much too cheerful for the occasion.

"Fernando, this is Matt and Joe, the two climbers who found the graves," Jodie said and then turned to the two hikers. "And this is Fernando Lopez, a private investigator in Santa Fe."

Fernando exchanged greetings with the two young men.

Jodie pointed to the two open graves, shallow pits no more than a couple of feet deep. Thankfully the two corpses were gone.

"That's where the mummies were found," Jodie said. "Forensics took the bodies yesterday evening. They'll be back today to search the area in the daylight."

Fernando nodded.

Jodie showed Fernando her cell phone. "Here's a photo of the two bodies when we uncovered them."

Fernando glanced at the photo and then turned his head. He'd seen enough. The two graves were side by side. The older mummy had turned black, its chest sunken. A bag of bones and rotting flesh. The more recent mummy disturbed him even more. The sheet winding had come loose on its right side and its arm reached up with clawed fingers as though trying to claw its way out of the grave. Looked like the woman had come back to life, like April at the Cerrillos Hills Visitor Center, but with no one to help her unwrap the sheet that bound her.

Fernando turned to the two young men. "How'd you find them?"

"Sure, we were on our way to camp in the Pecos but decided to stop here first and climb Devil's Throne," the older of the two said, a husky fellow with dark stubble on his ruddy face. "When we finished it was kind of late, so we decided to camp here for the night and go on to the Pecos today. We went to pitch our tent up here in the soft sand, but before we could I saw what looked like the roots of a dead plant sticking up out of the ground. I tried to pull it out so make room for the tent, but when I pulled on it the hand of a corpse came up out of the ground. I yelled when I realized I'd pulled on a dead person's fingers. Joe heard me yelling and came running up to see what was the matter. Good thing he did, because then he called to report the body. I was too freaked out to do anything."

Jodie stepped up. "We found the second grave when we got here. Forensics poked around and didn't find any others, but who knows? There could be more."

Fernando shook his head, not wanting to think about that. "So did you guys camp here last night then, after the bodies were found?" he asked Matt and Joe.

Joe, the younger of the two with a shock of blond hair falling across his forehead, blurted out, "No way, man! I refused. Creeped me out. I wanted to leave as soon as we gave our statements."

"Understandable," was all Fernando could think to say.

"I mean, she was alive, man," Joe continued. "She was trying to dig her way out of that grave. Like some Edgar Allen Poe story."

"Yeah, but it's a good thing you did find her," Matt said. "Otherwise we would have slept on the graves all night. Think about that. Imagine the bad karma that would bring."

"No thanks," Joe said.

Matt turned to Fernando. "So anyway we drove into Santa Fe and stayed at the Hampton Inn on the main drag there. We're on our way to the Pecos now. As soon as we finish here. I don't ever plan to come back to this place. I see why it's called Devil's Throne!"

Jodie nodded. "I have your statements and contact information, so you're free to go."

"Thanks," Matt said.

Fernando and Jodie watched the two climbers walk down to their green Subaru Forester. They rearranged their camping gear in the rear of the Forester. Then they climbed into the Forrester and buckled up. Waving, they drove off down the dirt road toward Cerrillos.

Jodie shook her head. "I don't know, Fernando. This case just gets worse by the day."

"Yeah, and its gonna keep getting worse until we find Anders," Fernando said.

"By the way, why is this place called Devil's Throne?" Jodie asked.

Fernando laughed. "How the hell would I know?"

27

Two days passed with no Anders sightings. The all points bulletin had produced no leads. The man seemed to have disappeared from the face of the earth. On the third day Fernando found himself at loose ends, tired of waiting around doing nothing. He needed to be active in order to keep from going to the dark place, as he called it. Estelle called it clinical depression and wanted him to get treatment, but the 'treatment' turned out to be nothing but medication, which turned him in to a zombie. No thank you. He preferred to deal with it his own way: by keeping busy and not looking back. One step ahead of the Grim Reaper.

He hadn't kept regular hours at his office, only stopping in to check his messages. Otherwise he stayed home or went for long walks on Acequia Madre or Canyon Road, anything to stay busy. He hadn't heard from Jodie since they left the shallow graves behind Devil's Throne. He knew her job kept her busy, so she didn't have the kind of down time that drove him crazy. He wasn't a patient man. One of his many faults, as pretty much everyone he'd ever known had pointed out.

This morning Fernando had worked in their garden for a while, until he got bored with that. Then he'd read the *Independent*, which always pissed him off for one reason or another. Then he'd watched CNN for a while, getting the latest doomsday news of the nation and the world. After lunch he got ready to go down to the office. If nothing else, he could visit with Ruby and maybe go to El Farol for Happy Hour this afternoon. Keeping busy, one way or another.

About to leave, Fernando's cell phone rang on he kitchen counter. He picked up the phone and saw Jodie's name on the screen. He clicked the accept button and answered.

"Fernando, he's still nearby, he hasn't run!" Jodie blurted out, a sense of urgency in her voice. "Did you hear me? He's still here!"

"I heard you," Fernando responded, irritated. "So how do you know this?"

"We just got a call from a bartender at the Mine Shaft Tavern in Madrid," Jodie said. "He recognized Anders from the APB description."

Surprised, Fernando said, "Madrid? That's just a few miles south of Cerrillos."

"That's what I mean, he's still here," Jodie said. "I'm on my way there now. You want to meet me?"

"I'm on my way," Fernando said and clicked off.

Finally! Some action.

Glad to be on the move again, Fernando buckled on his Smith & Wesson and hit the road. He raced around the Paseo to Cerrillos Road and turned off on State Road 14. By-passing the turn-off to Cerrillos, he continued south another five miles or so to Madrid, an old coal-mining town turned tourist trap. Once a ghost town, an influx of hippies back in the 1970s transformed the town into a counterculture, arts and crafts haven of sorts, adding an outer layer of bright colors to the gray, claptrap houses that had only intensified over the years.

Fernando drove into Madrid, seeing the old coal mine on his left, with a massive mound of black coal out front. On the right side of the road he saw a row of brightly painted galleries and arts and crafts shops, none brighter than the Cerrillos Turquoise store, a bulky wooden building with a steer skull over its front porch that sold everything from fine jewelry to handmade clothing. Painted in shades of red, blue, purple, and yellow, the building was a smorgasbord of color.

Just up the street he spotted the venerable Mine Shaft Tavern, a saloon and honkytonk popular with both locals and tourists. Painted brown with red trim, the sprawling Mine Shaft had a patio out back and a covered porch in front where its patrons could observe the surrounding Ortiz Mountains or watch the crowd of tourists meandering along Madrid's main drag. The Mine Shaft Tavern offered food, drink, music, and even a pool table for those so inclined.

Fernando pulled into the dirt lot out front of the Mine Shaft, next to Jodie's Cruiser. He jumped out of the Cherokee and walked past an antique tractor left over from Madrid's coal mining days. He climbed the steps to the funky porch and found a couple of old timers sitting at one of the tables nursing their beers. Both of them nodded to him as he walked into the dimly lit saloon. Classic funk, with hardwood floor, exposed vigas on the ceiling, and a Mine Shaft Tavern mural on one of the walls.

Jodie stood at the bar talking to an elderly bald man behind the bar. He had a long gray handlebar mustache and wore a paisley kerchief around his neck. Red lights behind the bar splashed the entire area, including Jodie and the bartender, in a reddish glare that made them look almost satanic.

Jodie introduced the bartender as Brian. Didn't give a last name.

"Brian, this is Fernando Lopez," Jodie said. "He's a private investigator helping on the case."

Brian nodded. "Well, like I was saying, I recognized this guy from the description. Plus I keep pretty close tabs on people roundabout here. We're a pretty close-knit community. I hadn't seen him before, so I knew he was an outsider. Same for the young woman he was with."

Jodie turned to Fernando. "Anders was with his moll."

"Melissa Vigil?" Fernando asked. "I can't say I'm surprised."

"Here, I shot a photo of them leaving," Brian said. He took a cellphone out of his back pocket and showed Jodie first and then Fernando. Sure enough, the photo captured Anders and Vigil getting into a blue Honda Civic: the car Melissa was driving when he'd seen her at the County Line Restaurant. That made sense. Driving her car they could stay under the radar. Anders must have ditched his Toyota pickup.

"How long ago did they leave?" Fernando asked.

Brian stroked his handlebar mustache. "I reckon about three hours. They stopped in for lunch and beers and then took off. Didn't say much to anyone. Kept to themselves."

Jodie shook her head. "Did he say why he was in Madrid? I mean, was he just passing through or what?"

"No, I don't think he was just passing through," Brian said. "I asked him whereabouts he was from, like I do every outsider who comes in here, and he said he was staying nearby. I was curious, but he wouldn't get any more specific than that. Just said he was staying near Cerro Chato."

"What's that?" Fernando said.

Brian pointed to the south. "That's the big old hill you see on the western side of the road down there. Must be about seven thousand feet above sea level. Maybe more. You can't miss it."

"How far down the road is it?" Jodie asked.

"I reckon it must be eight or ten miles as the crow flies, but a few more if you drive off the highway and climb up the hill, although I don't know why anyone would want to," Brian said.

"Why's that?" Jodie asked.

"Well, for one thing there ain't nothing to see on that hill," Brian said. "Just some ruins left by squatters, but they've been gone a long time. Last I heard nobody even knows who owns that land around Chato, whether it's some old Spanish land grant or government land managed by the Bureau of Land Management. It's a no man's land down there."

Jodie frowned, not liking what she was hearing. "Okay...but if you see them again, give us a call right away."

"Will do," Brian said. "I reckon they'll need to come into town for supplies, if they are staying somewhere on Chato."

Jodie nodded and headed for the door.

Fernando followed Jodie out of the saloon and down the porch steps to the parking lot.

Jodie stopped beside her cruiser. She leaned back against the trunk, arms folded across her chest. Fernando joined her, watching the tourists scurry from one shop to another along the street.

"What do you think?" Fernando asked, finally.

Jodie sighed. "We could post a watch here at the Mine Shaft Tavern if we had the personnel, but we don't. About all I can do is send a patrol down here a couple of times a day. Maybe we'll get lucky."

"What about Cerro Chato? You wanna check that out before we call it quits?" Fernando asked. "I have some ideas."

Jodie checked her wristwatch. "Whatever you say...because I got nothing."

Fernando motioned to the Cherokee. "Shall we take mine? It's four-wheel-drive, just in case we go off road."

Jodie shook her head. "No, we need to keep this official." She walked around and climbed into the driver's seat of the cruiser.

Before locking the doors of the Cherokee, Fernando took his binoculars out of the glove compartment. Then he joined Jodie.

As he opened the passenger's door Fernando heard Jodie mumble to herself, "Off road! I'm getting damn tired of chasing this guy."

"Copy that," Fernando said.

28

"What are we looking for, Melissa Vigil's car?" Jodie asked as she drove out of Madrid, passing the last of the gray, dilapidated houses clinging tentatively to the sides of the surrounding hills.

"Yeah, her blue Honda Civic," Fernando responded. "I'm thinking Anders ditched his Toyota pickup. Then when we get close to Cerro Chato, look for a driveway or a road that shows some evidence of recent activity. Tire tracks or whatever."

Jodie eased the cruiser down the road, keeping the speedometer well under 20 miles per hour. Rubber necking, they scanned the right side of the road for any sign of activity. On their way to Cerro Chato they passed several gated turn-offs with cattle guards and stopped at each one. All of them had primitive dirt roads that snaked up the hillsides and disappeared in a scattering of scraggly piñon and juniper trees, with no buildings or humans in sight. Looked like undeveloped grazing land. None of them seemed any more promising than any other.

When they reached the larger Cerro Chato, Jodie pulled over on the side of the highway and turned to Fernando. "Any ideas?"

Fernando climbed out of the cruiser and walked up the road a ways. From where he stood Chato looked even taller than the official seven thousand feet. He saw what looked like a narrow dirt road snaking its way halfway up the hillside to a flat parking area. The parking area snuggled up against a cliff composed of layers of sedimentary rock. He suddenly had an idea, so he walked back to the cruiser. Jodie hadn't moved from the driver's seat.

Fernando pointed to the dirt road. "See the narrow road? That goes up to a parking area halfway up the hill. How about we drive up as far as the parking area and then hike the rest of the way to the top of Chato? With my binoculars, we should be able to get an aerial view of all the lower hills."

Jodie stuck her head out of the driver's side window and glanced up at Chato. "I don't know, that's a big hill."

"Yeah, but from the parking area it's not that far to the top," Fernando said. "Maybe fifty, sixty yards, tops."

Jodie shrugged. "Okay, if you say so. Let's roll," she said.

After Fernando climbed inside the cruiser, Jodie eased back out on the highway. She proceeded slowly down to a pull-off where the dirt road up Cerro Chato began. Jodie paused at the entrance and looked at the winding road zig-zagging up the hillside. "I don't know, I don't see any recent tire tracks on the road," Jodie said. "It looks like loose sand. You think the cruiser will make it up there?"

Fernando laughed. "One way to find out."

With that, Jodie gunned the engine and stomped on the gas pedal. The cruiser skidded to the right, caught solid ground, and shot up the road scraping against an overgrown piñon tree. Like that, they plowed up the hill with the tires slipping and sliding and the big engine growling, occasionally grazing branches or bushes alongside the road.

When they reached the flat area beside the sedimentary rock formation, Jodie killed the engine and jumped out of the cruiser to inspect the damage caused by the branches. A few scratches in the paint, nothing too serious. She shook her head, not a happy camper.

"Normal wear and tear," Fernando said. "Comes with the job."

Jodie frowned. "Normal?"

Fernando pointed to a narrow trail that curved toward to the top of Cerro Chato. From a distance it looked like a ribbon, a brown slash in the dusty green hillside. He walked over to the trail and found both animal and human footprints, as well as narrow gauge tire tracks. Looked like dirt bikes had been tearing up the hill. As he came closer he saw the damage: mounds of brown dirt churned up by the motorized bikes. The brown scars pockmarked the hillside.

Jodie joined him at the trailhead. "Here, you forgot these," she said, handing him his binoculars. She scowled at the churned up hillside. "I hate those dirt bikes. They should be illegal."

"Yeah, but then you'd have to enforce it," Fernando said.

Jodie didn't respond. She took off up the trail walking at her usual speeds: fast and faster.

Fernando followed, but he didn't try to keep up with her. He knew from experience that he couldn't. The woman was a former college athlete and thirty years younger. So why bother?

Like Jodie, he hated the damn dirt bikes, so he tried not to look at the damage they'd done. He fell farther and farther behind Jodie as they climbed the hill. By the time he reached the top, she was standing at the far northern edge of Chato looking back toward Madrid.

"You can just see the top of the old coal mine from here," Jodie said, pointing north.

"Let's take a look," Fernando replied. He adjusted his binoculars and scanned the hills between Chato and Madrid one at a time. The first hill looked clean, as did the second, but when he came to the third hill, one of those with a gated fence and cattle guard out front, he spotted a well feeding a galvanized steel water tank. Located on a flat area near the top of the hill, the tank would supply water to grazing cattle. He scanned the rest of the hill but saw no livestock or other animals near the tank. What he did see made him smile.

In a hollow just below the tank he spotted a wooden structure and a small blue sedan. That would be Melissa Vigil's Honda Civic.

"Well, well, look what we have here,' Fernando said. He passed the binoculars to Jodie. "Take a look at the third hill over toward Madrid."

Jodie raised the binoculars. She scanned and then stopped. "You can run, but you can't hide," she muttered to herself. "What's that building next to the car? My eyes aren't as good as they used to be."

Laughing, Fernando took back the binoculars. "You actually have a physical problem, I can't believe it."

"Yeah, my optometrist tells me I need glasses, but I haven't bothered," Jodie said. "Don't look so pleased."

Fernando took another look at the building. He recognized the structure as a round wooden yurt no doubt built years ago by one of the squatters mentioned by the bartender at the Mine Shaft Tavern.

"It's a yurt, probably built by one of the squatters," Fernando said.

"What's a yurt?" Jodie shot back. "Pardon me, but I didn't grow up in the age of hippies living in teepees and yurts."

Fernando laughed, even though her comment rubbed him the wrong way. He had indeed grown up in the age of hippies living in teepees, and yes, he did know a little something about yurts. In fact, he knew someone who built a yurt back in the day: Antonio. The big man built his yurt in the Pecos Wilderness as a temporary shelter following his divorce. Later he built the cabin he now inhabited, a more elaborate structure that he ordered from Colorado and assembled by himself.

Sighing, Fernando said, "It's a portable, round structure that can be assembled and reassembled. All you need is some kind of base to built the deck on, cement or even rocks. This one's made out of wooden slats held upright by a compression ring that encircles the slats. The roof rafters are held up by another tension band that opposes the force of the roof ribs. They're popular with nomadic tribes in Central Asia...and hippies. You can buy yurt kits from Colorado and other Western states for a few thousand dollars. Then you just have to assemble them."

Jodie stared at him as though he had spoken in Russian or Outer Mongolian. "I have no idea what you're talking about. Compression ring, tension band, what the hell is that?"

"Just wait. You'll see when we get there," Fernando said, turning away and heading for the trail.

Jodie passed him halfway down the trail. He said nothing. She didn't look back.

29

Jodie was standing next to her cruiser with the driver's door open waiting for him by the time Fernando made it back to the parking area next to the sedimentary rock formation. "Nice you could make it," she said.

Fernando laughed. "You wouldn't leave me out here, would you?"

"No, but only because I need back up," Jodie said, smiling.

Fernando climbed into the cruiser and buckled up tight for the rough ride down to the highway at the bottom of the hill. Jodie backed up gingerly and then spun around in the loose dirt. She eased out onto the dirt road and applied the gas. The cruiser spun out of control for a moment, but Jodie managed to wrestle the steering wheel this way and that and get the big car back on track. The cruiser slid, skidded, and slid some more down the winding dirt road before crash-landing in a large stand of chamisa alongside the highway.

"Don't say anything," Jodie said.

Fernando didn't.

Jodie backed up, tires spinning, and managed to disentangle the front bumper from the chamisa bush, which was already beginning to turn yellow. Another sign of the change of seasons. Then she eased across a shallow ditch and out onto the highway.

Once on State Road 14, Jodie drove quickly to the hill where they'd seen the yurt and the livestock tank. She turned into the gated entrance and pulled up at the closed gate. She switched off the engine and set the brake. Then she sat there staring at the gate for a few seconds before asking, "What do you think, should we try to open the gate and drive in?"

Fernando shook his head. "No, let's walk, keep the element of surprise. We didn't see Anders' car, so who knows what we'll find. He might not even be here."

Jodie nodded her agreement.

They climbed out of the cruiser and walked to the metal gate. On the other side of the gate a winding dirt road disappeared into a thick cover of piñon and juniper, much like Cerro Chato. From where they stood they couldn't see the yurt or Melissa Vigil's car, but they did see fresh tire tracks on the other side of the gate. Jodie pointed to the tire tracks.

"I see them," Fernando said.

Jodie walked up to the gate and found it chained and padlocked on the other side of the metal gate. She turned and walked around the gate into the adjoining ditch, where a barbed wire fence attached to the gate. She stepped through the barbed wire strands and then held open the strands for Fernando.

Before proceeding, Fernando checked his Smith & Wesson to make sure it was loaded. It was. If needed, he had additional rounds in a leather pouch on his belt.

Jodie led the way up the hill. They avoided the road. Instead they crept up through the gnarly piñon and juniper trees, avoiding the cactus and any dead branches or plants that would make a noise if stepped on. Not knowing exactly where the yurt was located, they hiked straight up the hill, looking from side to side. On the way up Fernando had to stop for a pee. Jodie waited impatiently for him to finish. Just moments after they resumed hiking Jodie stopped and froze.

"Shhh...I hear something," Jodie whispered. "Someone's walking through the trees up there."

Fernando took out his Smith & Wesson and waited. Long seconds passed as the footsteps grew louder. Jodie removed the Glock from her duty belt and pointed it at the trees.

Suddenly a fallen tree branch snapped loudly. Fernando jumped to one side, taking cover behind a half-buried rock. Jodie sank to her knees, her Glock steady in her hand.

Then they saw it: a cow. A fucking cow!

Jodie chuckled and said, "Let's follow the cow. It seems to know where it's going, probably to the water tank."

So they crept along behind the cow as it meandered up the hillside, not paying any attention to the two puny humans following along behind. The cow was imperturbable, oblivious to its surroundings. It trudged on through the bushes and trees with only one thing in mind—to get where it was going. That turned out to be the water tank, as Jodie had speculated. They saw the tank ahead of them as they approached the top of the hill, a metal tank about ten feet in diameter stained algae green and black from years of heavy use.

The cow went directly to the tank and began slobbering up water. When they approached, the cow turned to look at them for a split second and then, disinterested, turned back to the tank and began slobbering water again.

Jodie motioned to her right. Fernando followed her across the top of the hill. From the summit they looked down on the hollow they had seen with the binoculars. The yurt stood in the center of the hollow about thirty yards from where they stood, its back to them. Built with rough-cut lumber, now aged a dark gray color, the round structure sagged in the middle as though its roof were about to collapse inward. Even some of the sideboards of the yurt sagged out unevenly, like broken ribs. The structure looked at least twenty years old, maybe more. An eyesore.

Fernando crouched in the sagebrush and studied the layout of the hollow. He saw Melissa Vigil's blue Honda Civic parked directly in front of the yurt over by the dirt road. On the far left side of the hollow a tiny wooden shed had been built near an arroyo, most likely an outhouse. Further down he saw Anders' red Toyota pickup partially hidden in the arroyo. Anders had either pushed or driven the pickup into the arroyo and then covered it with a thick layer of brush and brown tumbleweeds. You had to be close-up in order to see the truck under its layer of debris.

Jodie pointed to the Honda Civic. "They must be here somewhere."

Fernando nodded. "Probably in the yurt."

"Why don't you go down to the right...I'll go to the left," Jodie said.

"Okay," Fernando said.

As instructed, Fernando moved down the incline to the right of the yurt. He moved slowly while carefully watching where he stepped, not wanting to make unnecessary noise. Coming closer, he noticed a trash dump behind the yurt filled with rusted tin cans, broken glass, and twisted metal. He also noticed that the yurt had no interior liner, so he could see light in the tiny spaces between the slats. He looked for shadows or movement in the gaps that would indicate someone was inside, but saw none. When he came up behind the yurt, he stopped and listened for any movement inside or out front of the yurt. He heard only wind whistling in the trees and a distant bird calling plaintively.

Fernando had lost sight of Jodie, who was somewhere on the other side of the yurt. So he had to make the decision for himself. He decided to move.

With his Smith & Wesson in hand he crept around the yurt to the front entrance. Instead of a door, he found a torn, frayed piece of canvas nailed to the top of the doorframe. He saw Jodie coming around the other side of the yurt, so he waited for her to join him and then flung back the canvas curtain.

Fernando and Jodie stood shoulder to shoulder with guns drawn, staring at the interior of the yurt. Anders and Vigil were not there. So where were they? That was the question.

They moved to the back of the yurt, finding a foam pad and two sleeping bags, a Coleman stove and other camping equipment, and a stack of cardboard boxes likely containing Anders' medicinal herbs and witchcraft paraphernalia. Clearly Anders had packed up quickly before he'd torched and abandoned his pit-house behind Devil's Throne. Now this, a dilapidated yurt in the middle of nowhere. Anders was running out of places to hide.

Suddenly they heard a noise out front. A split second later the canvas ripped away from the door opening.

Sven Anders stood before them holding a pistol in his hand. He looked tired and haggard, with murky splotches on his pale face and wild, unkempt black hair down to his shoulders. His gun resembled Jodie's 9 mm Glock. "Why do you keep following me? Haven't you learned your lesson?"

Steady as ever, Jodie answered mater-of-factly, "Because you killed four people, maybe more."

Anders shook his head. "They died for science. How many times do I have to explain. My research is more important than any individual life."

"Says who? You?" Fernando erupted, tired of listening to this arrogant prick. "What gives you the right to play God?"

"Science gives me the right. God is just what we call science."

"Bullshit!" Fernando shouted. "What you do isn't science, it's voodoo witchcraft nonsense. You're nothing but a murderer."

Anders shook his head. "I'm going to have to kill you now."

"There's two of us, one of you," Jodie said coldly. She had nerves of steel. She never lost her cool.

"Doesn't matter," Anders responded. "Even if you kill me, I will come back to life. I have my apprentice here to administer the resurrection drug."

Jodie moved slowly away from Fernando, so Anders would not have a single target. "Now drop your gun," she ordered. "You're under arrest for the murder of Fidel Rodriguez and—"

As Jodie spoke they heard footsteps approaching outside the yurt. A split second later Melissa Vigil appeared next to Anders in the doorway, hiking up her shorts and underwear. Her skimpy shorts and tight T-shirt made her look very young, like a teenager.

"It's bad enough that I have to pee in that damn outhouse—" Melissa started to complain and then stopped when she saw the standoff, the three of them with weapons drawn.

Instantly Anders threw his left arm around Melissa's neck and put her in a choke- hold. Melissa screamed, "Oww...lemme go, you fucker!"

"Now drop your weapons, or I'll kill her," Anders said to Fernando and Jodie.

Melissa continued to struggle against Anders.

"You're making a big mistake, Anders," Jodie said. "Turn yourself in now before you get yourself in deeper trouble."

"I'll kill her!" Anders shouted, putting his pistol against Melissa's forehead. "Drop your weapons. Now!"

Fernando placed his Smith & Wesson on the floor.

Jodie lowered her Glock, staring at Anders. Finally she placed the pistol on the floor.

Without saying another word, Anders dragged Melissa away from the yurt and over toward her Honda Civic.

Jodie grabbed her Glock and moved to the doorway of the yurt, hearing the Honda's doors open and close. She took aim at the Honda as it drove off down the driveway. "Shit!" she said. "Shit! I can't get a clean shot."

Fernando squeezed past Jodie and ran outside, jogging down the road to a rise that overlooked a cut-back, thinking he might have a clean shot from above. No such luck. The car had already disappeared down the hillside by the time he reached the rise. The gate at the bottom of the hill was wide open.

Jodie walked up behind him. The two of them watched a cloud of brown dust dissipate over the road.

30

Running down the hill was faster than going up but harder on the knees. By the time they reached the gate Fernando was out of breath and gasping for air. His knees hurt like hell. On the other hand Jodie didn't seem much affected. She waited for him to get his breath and called her station and ordered an APB on the Blue Honda Civic. She'd taken a photo of the Civic's license on her way down to the yurt.

When she finished the call, Jodie came over to join Fernando. She checked her wristwatch. "Well, it's been a good half hour since they took off. They could be in Albuquerque by now or halfway to the state line, either Colorado or Texas. What do you think?"

Fernando shook his head. "Your call. I got nothing."

Jodie kicked at the loose gravel around the gate. "Yeah, I guess we'll have to wait until the APB turns up a lead. I'm so sick of chasing this guy."

"I don't know what else we can do," Fernando said.

"So why did you drop your gun back at the yurt?" Jodie asked. "We could have had him back there."

"He was going to shoot the girl," Fernando said. "What else could we do under the circumstances?"

"I was about to shoot the bastard between the eyes, that's what we could have done," Jodie countered. "We had him two against one. You folded too soon."

Fernando stared at her for a few moments and then shook his head. He walked to the cruiser and climbed into the front passenger's seat without saying a word. No one had ever accused him of folding too soon. But let it go, he told himself. Don't get into an argument with Jodie. It's her case.

Jodie joined him in the cruiser, slamming the door shut a little harder than she needed to. "I'll drop you off at your office...unless you can think of something else we can do to catch up to Anders."

Fernando bit his tongue.

Jodie started the cruiser, backed up, and eased up to the highway, intending to turn left toward Santa Fe. She flashed her turn signal and hit the gas pedal.

"Stop!" Fernando shouted and grabbed the wheel.

Jodie slammed on the brakes, lurching them forward. "Why? Why do you want me to stop?" she asked.

Fernando pointed to the right. A couple of hundred feet down State Road 14 South stood Melissa Vigil, all by her lonesome. She had her thumb sticking out, trying to hitch a ride.

Jodie sighed. "I don't believe it."

"He must have dumped her," Fernando said.

"Go get her," Jodie said.

Fernando opened the car door and jumped out. He waved at Melissa and started walking down the highway. When she saw him coming, she cursed and gave him the finger.

Just then a car approached from the south. Melissa moved to the center of the highway waving her thumb at the oncoming car. The surprised driver honked at Melissa and swerved onto the side of the road to avoid hitting her. Instead, he hit a roadside sign advertising the Mine Shaft Tavern on the other side of the road, sending the wooden sign into the air. Exploding into splinters, the pieces of wood floated in the air and then landed behind the car. The driver didn't bother to stop. He righted the vehicle and proceeded down the highway without looking back.

"What are you doing here?" Fernando asked as he approached Melissa.

Melissa looked at him, frowning. "I'm hitchhiking to Albuquerque. The asshole kicked me out of my own car. He said he'd pick me up in Albuquerque in a couple of days."

"Come with us," Fernando said, holding out his hand. "We need your statement. Then we can take you to Albuquerque."

"Go fuck yourself," Melissa said. She turned away and started walking down the highway away from him.

Fernando followed, entreating her to come with him. When he realized she wasn't about to turn around, he grabbed her from behind and lifted her up in his arms.

"Put me down, you big oaf!" she screamed.

Fernando carried her, kicking and screaming, back to the cruiser.

Laughing, Jodie shook her head when they arrived and climbed out of the car to meet them. "Now that's a sight you don't often see."

"She's all yours," Fernando said, setting Melissa down in front of

Jodie, as if the young woman was an offering of sorts.

"Get in the car," Jodie said to Melissa. "We're taking you to the station. We need a statement from you. After that, we'll see what the Chief wants to do."

Melissa shoved Fernando away from her and screamed at Jodie. "No! I'm on my way to Albuquerque, bitch!"

That was the wrong thing to say to the wrong person. The young girl did not know who she was messing with. Fernando stepped back, out of Jodie's way.

Furious, her face fiery red, Jodie grabbed Melissa and spun the tiny girl around facing her. Then she poked the girl in the chest repeatedly. Hard. "Listen, missy, I don't know if you were Anders' accomplice or his prisoner or what, but you're coming with us to Santa Fe whether you like it or not. I don't care if I have to handcuff you and throw you in the trunk, now shut your mouth and get in the car before I lose my temper and do something I'll regret!"

"Owww!" Melissa cried out with each poke. "You're mean."

"Ha! You have no idea," Jodie said.

Fernando couldn't help himself. "It's true. You don't."

Jodie gave him a dirty look.

Rubbing her sore chest, Melissa climbed into the back seat of the cruiser and pouted.

Jodie slammed the door closed and walked around to the driver's seat. She waited for Fernando to get in and then looked at Melissa in the rear view mirror. "So where's Anders?"

Melissa made a face. "I don't know where he is. He said he had to get more supplies and that he was going to meet me in Albuquerque in a couple of days. That's all he said."

"More supplies?" Jodie asked.

"That's what he said," Melissa repeated.

Then it hit Fernando like a bolt of lightning. "No problem, I know where he's going."

Both women turned to look at him.

"Gabe Rivera," Fernando said.

3 1

"Gabe Rivera? Who's Gabe Rivera?" Jodie asked, before pulling out on the highway.

"He's the *curandero* I told you about," Fernando said. "He has a medicinal herb shop in Galisteo. I think it's where Anders has been getting his supply of Wolfsbane and some of the other stuff. Stealing them would be more accurate."

Jodie looked in the rear view mirror and asked Melissa, "Do you know this Rivera guy?"

"Never heard of him," Melissa said.

Jodie sighed. "Okay, but it'll take some time to get back to Santa Fe and swing over to State Road forty-one."

"Actually, there's a short cut," Fernando said. "Take County Road Forty-two about five miles north of Cerrillos. Look for the next unmaintained road on your right, you can't miss it. If you come to the San Marcos Arroyo, you've gone too far."

Jodie glanced at Fernando. "How do you know all these back roads?"

Fernando laughed. "I grew up here. I know this area like the back of my hand."

"Whatever you say," Jodie said, easing out on the highway and heading toward Cerrillos. Minutes later they passed the Galisteo River and the turn-off to Cerrillos. Jodie slowed down after a couple of miles.

Fernando watched carefully for County Road 42. He remembered the road as being difficult to find. The Galisteo basin was criss-crossed by county and unmaintained roads of one kind or another, including Wolf Road. But when he spotted the San Marcos Arroyo ahead, he pointed to the unmarked gravel road to their right.

Jodie hesitated, but made the turn finally. Driving through the empty expanse of desert, she said, "This is a no man's land out here."

"Yeah, lotta BLM and State Trust land until you come to Galisteo," Fernando said.

They crossed the Cañada de la Cueva and a few miles later the Burlington, Northern and Santa Fe railroad tracks before driving into Galisteo. Fernando directed Jodie past the church to the left-hand turn leading to Gabe Rivera's herb shop. They drove into the rolling mesas of the Galisteo Basin, bouncing up and down in the cruiser. Tumbleweed blew across the dirt and gravel road and caught in the barbed wire fences lining the road, carving out parcels of land as dry as dust. Hard to believe any animal, wild or domestic, could find enough to graze on in such inhospitable terrain.

They swung to the right over a small rise. From the top they spotted Gabe's roadside shack snuggled in a hollow with its back up against an earthen bank. Jodie shook her head when she saw the dilapidated building. Gray, unpainted wood with a cupola on top, no less. Something you might see in one of those Wild West ghost towns in Arizona, where tourists came to watch—and pay for—re-enactments of famous gunfights.

Fernando pointed to the right side of the shack.

"I see it," Jodie said, eyeing the blue Honda Civic parked off to the side of the shack, between it and an old, empty corral. The corral, or what was left of it, looked as old as Gabe's shack. "Jesus, this place looks like it's right out of a movie set—like the one where that woman cinematographer was accidentally shot and killed."

"Bonanza Creek Ranch, that was the movie set for Rust, the movie you mention," Fernando added.

Jodie stopped on the side of the road, about twenty or thirty yards from the shack. From where they were parked they saw no one. The Honda Civic looked empty, which meant Anders must be inside the shack.

Jodie jumped out of the cruiser and opened the rear door on the passenger side of the car. "Okay, hold out your hands," she said to Melissa, taking the cuffs off her duty belt.

"Awww, come on, you're not gonna cuff me?" Melissa asked.

Jodie grabbed Melissa's right wrist and cuffed it. When Melissa tried to keep the other hand away from her, Jodie yanked on the cuffs until Melissa cried out. "Ouch! Okay!" the young woman said.

Jodie snapped on the other cuff and said, "Stay in the car. If you don't, I'll put you in the trunk and keep you there until we get to Santa Fe."

Melissa wisely kept her mouth shut.

Jodie took the lead, walking through dead weeds in the ditch to get over to a sandy path leading to the shack. With her service weapon in hand, Jodie motioned for Fernando to check out the Honda Civic and then made a bee-line for the rickety porch.

Fernando took out his Smith & Wesson and circled around the shack to where the Honda was parked. He saw a backpack and a large duffel bag on the back seat, but nothing else in the car. He was about to try to open the trunk when he heard Jodie shout in front of the shack.

"Drop it!" Jodie shouted.

Suddenly shots rang out: Crack! Crack!

Fernando recognized the sound of bullets hitting wood. He raced around to the front and found Jodie crouching on the wooden deck, off to the side of the rusted screen door. She motioned for him to get down, so he ducked and huddled against the steps leading to the porch.

"Anders is holding the old man's son captive," Jodie said. "He says he'll kill the son if we try to arrest him."

Back to that again. The hostage standoff. Something had to give.

"Let me talk to him," Fernando said.

"Go ahead...before I have to shoot him," Jodie said.

Fernando crawled onto the porch, remaining on his hands and knees while he tried to peer inside the screen door. He saw the long wooden counter and behind it the shelves stocked with glass jars of medicinal herbs, but no sign of Anders or Gabe's son, Tomas.

"Anders? Can you hear me?" Fernando shouted. "Come out now before anyone else gets hurt. There's been enough bloodshed. The sheriff here will talk to the District Attorney and try to get you a plea deal."

No response from Anders.

"She'll put in a good word for you. What do you say?" Fernando continued, biting his tongue. The chances of Jodie ever putting in a good word for Anders were slim to none and Slim was long gone.

"Leave, all of you, or I'll shoot this guy!" Anders shouted back. "I'm trying to do my research, why do you keep bothering me. Get out of here! Now!"

With that Anders punctuated his orders with a gunshot: Crack! The bullet ripped through the wooden porch floor inches from Fernando, who rolled to his right, away from the screen door.

"Put down the gun and come out with your hands up, Anders," Jodie ordered. "You're surrounded here. There's no way out. This is the end of the line."

"Hah!" Ander shouted. "I've taken my Sanjeevani. I have no fear of death."

Fernando heard scuffling sounds from inside the shack. Then

heavy steps. Someone was moving slowly toward the screen door.

Suddenly Anders violently kicked the screen door off its hinges. The crumpled door rattled on the wooden porch.

Tomas came out first, a short, dark-haired man wearing a blood-stained white T-shirt and jeans. He looked to be in his fifties, but there was no way to tell for sure because his face was covered in blood from a deep gash on his forehead.

Anders pushed Tomas from behind, using him as a shield. He held his Glock against Tomas' head, as he had done with Melissa earlier. His eyes darted from side to side. He looked possessed.

Possessed by what, Fernando wondered.

"Stand back!" Anders ordered.

Fernando stepped down and to the side of the porch.

Jodie stood up and held her ground, her service revolver pointed at Anders.

The moment seemed to freeze, with the four of them stuck in place and in time. They stared at each other. No one spoke.

Then Anders began to move, pushing Tomas ahead of him one small step after another. In the silence of the moment their footsteps echoed on the wooden porch. Ever closer to the steps down.

Suddenly Fernando saw old Gabe approaching from his house next door. He made his way slowly, quietly behind the shack and then peeked out from around the left corner of the porch. He held a shotgun in his hand, a pained expression on his ancient face, as though he'd been in this situation before and knew he would regret what he was about to do.

The old man raised his shotgun.

Then everything seemed to happen all at once.

"Now, Tomas!" Gabe shouted.

Tomas ducked and dived head-first off the porch.

Anders turned to face Gabe.

Gabe pulled the trigger: Boom!

The shotgun blast lifted Anders off the porch. He landed flat on his back next to Tomas. Anders tried to raise his head and shoulders but fell backwards in the dust and lay still, his eyes wide open and a look of surprise fixed on his face.

Fernando scrambled to his feet but kept his distance, giving Jodie room to inspect Anders. Anders chest was a mass of mangled flesh and oozing blood.

Jodie took one look at Anders and didn't bother to check for a pulse.

A moment later Gabe came out from behind the corner. His long white hair and milky blue eyes made him look like the Grim Reaper himself. "Did I wing him...or did I kill the sonofabitch?"

Neither Fernando nor Jodie answered.

Tomas scurried away from the body on his hands and knees. Then he stood and dusted off his clothing. "You killed him, pops."

Gabe nodded solemnly. He hobbled around the porch and stopped to stare at Anders' lifeless body. After a few seconds he shuffled off into the shack, a skeleton wrapped in loose-fitting clothes. The old man cursed when he saw the damage inside the shack.

Jodie sighed. "I'll call Forensics."

Fernando nodded.

Jodie pointed to the cruiser. "You wanna go after the girl?"

Fernando turned and saw the empty cruiser. Melissa Vigil had abandoned ship and once again was walking down the road, this time toward the village of Galisteo. In no great hurry, she could have been out for an afternoon stroll except that she held her handcuffed hands out in front of her. Not running as though she were trying to escape, just strolling down the road.

Leaving Jodie to make her call, Fernando walked quickly to the cruiser. Once on the dirt road he half walked, half ran down the narrow lane after Melisa, who ignored him until he reached out and grabbed her shoulder.

"Hey—take it easy," she said. "What are you, some kind of pedophile?"

"Pedophile? What in the hell are you talking about?" Fernando said, getting his breath.

"Grabbing me and everything," Melissa said.

"Because you're running away!" Fernando shouted, exasperated. "Now get back to the car."

Melissa shook her head. "No thanks, I'll just hitch-hike down to Albuquerque."

"That does it," Fernando said. He came up behind Melissa and picked her up and once again carried her kicking and screaming toward the car.

"Help! Rape!" she screamed, but there was nobody in hearing distance. By the time they made it back to the cruiser she'd given up the act and resumed her stony, sullen attitude.

Fernando dropped her in the dirt and let her sit on her ass while he opened the door of the cruiser.

"Owww, you bastard!" Melissa replied.

Fernando picked her up again and tossed her in the back seat.

Hearing the commotion, Jodie walked up to the cruiser and opened the trunk. Then she came around to Melissa. "You try to run again and I swear to God, I'll put you in the trunk."

Melissa pouted. "You guys are mean."

32

By the time they made it back to Santa Fe the sun had already begun to sink behind the western horizon. Jodie dropped off Fernando at his office on Canyon Road, promising to keep him informed of further developments. He saluted as she drove off with Melissa Vigil sitting in the back of the cruiser, a sour look on her face. Still pouting. Melissa hadn't said a word since being told Anders was dead and didn't seem particularly concerned about it either way. Hard to figure.

Fernando was hot, tired, and too damned old for a long day like this. He walked down the gravel path to his office and unlocked the door, not bothering to remove the 'Closed' sign in the window. He'd had enough of people and their problems today, thank you very much. He took a Modelo out of his mini-frig, opened the bottle, and collapsed in his desk chair.

Beginning to relax, Fernando helped himself to another Modelo. He knew he should head for home and dinner with Estelle. But he also knew that she was almost certainly pissed since he hadn't called earlier to tell her he would be late, so why bother? Plus he had one task remaining before he could call it a day. He had to call Dorothy to tell her the news: they had found and killed the man who murdered Fidel. She needed to know. For closure.

"Hello, this is Dorothy," she answered.

"Hi Dorothy, it's Fernando," he said. "I finally have some news. We tracked down the man who killed Fidel—Sven Anders is his name. We caught up with him in Galisteo. He's dead now. He won't hurt anyone else."

Dorothy did not respond.

"Are you still there?" Fernando asked.

"Yes, I heard you," she said. "Did you kill him?"

"No, actually the owner of a store he was trying to rob shot and killed him," Fernando said. "Anders took a hostage, but the owner of the store got a clear shot. It was over quickly."

Again Dorothy did not immediately respond. She sighed. "Funny, but I've waited for days to hear this. I so much wanted revenge. I just wanted Fidel's killer to die a cruel death. But now, I don't know...I just feel an emptiness. Revenge just seems like more of the same. More killing. I'm sorry...I should feel grateful, and I do really. I'm just sad for everyone. Does that make any sense?"

"Perfect sense," Fernando said. "I just wanted you to know that we caught the killer."

"I know, you're a good friend, Fernando," Dorothy said and clicked off.

Fernando finished his second Modelo and then went home to a cold dinner. Estelle had already retired for the night. He sat in the kitchen by himself brooding about Fidel's death and Dorothy's sadness. Then he brooded about Melissa Vigil's attitude, her seeming lack of interest in the death of Anders, which called into question the extent of her involvement with Anders' so-called research. Just what was her relationship with Anders then?

He sat at the kitchen table for over an hour waiting for Jodie to call with further developments. She didn't call, not that night and not the next day. In fact, days went by without hearing from her.

Finally one afternoon after he'd just returned from lunch at El Farol, he heard footsteps on the gravel path outside his office. Moments later Jodie breezed into his office without knocking. She helped herself to a chair and said, "Sorry I haven't gotten back to you sooner. We've had a series of shootings and armed robberies. Been a nightmare, because we're still short-staffed. It's even worse since another deputy resigned last week."

"Sorry to hear that," Fernando said.

"These days all the young people want to be on the other side of the law, selling drugs and guns," Jodie said. "The country's gone to hell, Fernando."

Fernando nodded. "Sometimes it seems that way. So what happened to Melissa Vigil and the Anders investigation?"

Jodie frowned. "No surprise there. Forensics matched Anders' fingerprints and DNA with what they found on all three victims, the two women mummies and Fidel Rodriguez. Anders is definitely our man."

"What about Melissa Vigil?" Fernando asked.

Jodie shook her head. "That's a long story. We held her overnight for questioning. She denied being in cahoots with Anders, of course. Said she didn't even like him because he held her prisoner and raped her, but when I asked why she shot at you that day at the pit-house, she had no answer. The District Attorney, who's a hard ass, is doubtful we have much of a case against her because we have little to no hard evidence. Looks like he'll offer her a plea deal: six months probation on the condition that she lives under the supervision of her parents."

"Hah! She'll love that, I've met her mother," Fernando said, even though six months probation was pretty much what he expected.

"But I gave her a piece of my mind before we released her," Jodie continued. "I sat her down and told her to get her act together and make something of herself. I also told her to lay off men, especially men like Sven Anders. They're more trouble than they're worth, which isn't saying much since most men are worthless. Present company excepted, of course."

"Of course," Fernando repeated. "So where is she now?"

"She was discharged in the custody of her parents," Jodie said. "They drove up from Albuquerque to pick her up."

"What do you think?" Fernando asked. "You think she was working with Anders?"

Jodie laughed. "I think she's guilty as hell. Of course she was working with Anders, but in what capacity we'll probably never know. The D.A. just doesn't think he can prove it."

Fernando did not respond.

"Plus the parents have already lawyered up," Jodie said. "One of your old friends."

Fernando's spirits sank. "Not Raoul Garcia?"

"Oh yes, none other than the great Raoul Garcia," Jodie said. "Raoul's already floating the idea that Vigil is suffering from Stockholm Syndrome. You know, where the hostage starts to side with the captor."

Raoul Garcia had been a fiery Chicano lawyer back in the seventies and eighties, defending a rag-tag lot of hippies and revolutionaries and virtually never losing a case. He was old now, too old to hang with hipsters and revolutionaries, so he usually defended rich fucks accused of white collar crimes, but his reputation was such that every lawyer or prosecutor feared coming up against him.

"Yeah, Steve Chabot wouldn't go up against Raoul," Fernando said. "Not with that case."

"Exactly," Jodie said. "So tell me, you have two grown daughters, what's with this Melissa Vigil? Where does she get that privileged, smart-ass attitude?"

"Like you said, privilege...I guess," Fernando said. "What I don't understand is why she was attracted to Anders."

"Lotta women are attracted to bad boys, Fernando. That's no mystery."

Fernando shook his head. He supposed she was right. Sadly.

"Anyway, I just wanted to give you an update," Jodie said.

Fernando saluted.

Jodie walked to the door and stopped. She turned around and said, "Remember what Anders said just before the old man shot him? That he'd taken his Sanjeevani and would come back to life?"

"I remember," Fernando said.

"Well, he didn't," Jodie said and walked out of his office.

33

One morning a week later Fernando came to a decision. He decided to retire once and for all from his work as a private investigator and close down his office. Estelle was right, the time had come to call it quits. Sitting at his desk, Fernando scanned the contents of his office. He would have to move his desk and chairs, his file cabinet, and his mini refrigerator. Unless Ruby wanted to keep the furniture for her next tenant. Better yet. That would be the least he could do to repay her for not charging him rent these past few years.

He hadn't seen Ruby's car when he drove into their parking lot this morning, which was unusual. She almost always opened her gallery next door on time. So he ducked outside to check and saw her Honda Accord parked next to his Cherokee. He didn't bother to lock his office. Instead, he walked around to the front of her gallery and stepped up on the porch, where he found Ruby's keys still in the front door. He grabbed the keys and walked inside.

"Ruby?" he called out

"Yeah, I'm back here, trying to make some coffee," she answered from the back room.

Fernando found her fussing with a Keurig machine. "What's the problem?"

"The damn thing is too slow, that's the problem," Ruby said. She looked disheveled this morning, not her usual knockout. Wearing jeans and a T-shirt, she had dark circles under her eyes and frizzy hair that stuck up every which way.

"Hard night?" Fernando asked.

Ruby nodded. "Goddamn Blaine was hassling me about Jimmy's paintings again. He kept buying me margaritas, hoping I would give in. I lost track at five or six, I can't remember. I used to be able to keep up with the bastard, but I've lost a step. Go figure!"

Fernando laughed. "Yeah, tell me about it. That's kind of why I'm here. I've decided to retire."

"You?" Ruby asked, surprised. She spilled some of her coffee on the counter and cursed. Then she took a sip of the steaming black liquid, her hands shaking. Sighing, she said, "You want me to make you a cup?"

He glanced at the spilled coffee dripping off the counter to the floor. "No, I'm good."

"So what's this about retiring?" Ruby asked. "You can't retire until I do and that's like never gonna happen. Ever! What would I do without you? Just knowing you're down in your office, my protector."

"Thanks, but it's like you say, I've lost a step," Fernando said, shaking his head. "I'm tired. I just need to take it easy for a while."

"Hah! Pussy!" Ruby chastised him. "Suck it up like the rest of us."

"Plus you'd be able to rent your garage to a paying tenant," Fernando said. "You could actually collect rent!"

Ruby thought about that for a moment. "Hmmm. Now that's a thought. Thing is, what kind of business would move into such a small space? Only thing I could think of would be another damn real estate agent. That's all we need. They've already ruined Canyon Road, it's starting to look like a Disneyland theme park."

Fernando frowned. "Don't start on gentrification. You know I agree with you, but that's water under the bridge. Our side lost."

"See!" Ruby said. "I need you here for moral support. We're old soldiers. You understand. I can't have some Sotheby's asshole next door."

Fernando shrugged.

"Tell you what," Ruby said, pausing a moment to think. "Leave all your stuff in the office. I won't touch a thing. I'll keep the place available, just in case you change your mind, which I'm sure you will."

Fernando started to reply, but Ruby raised her hands, cutting him off. "Discussion over. I'm keeping your options open."

Fernando thanked Ruby again and sat in a nearby chair. "I'll take that cup of coffee, after all."

Later, after they'd finished their coffees, Ruby's first customer of the day walked into her gallery. Fernando took the opportunity to make a quick exit. Though he resisted at first, he'd come around to the idea of keeping his options open. Knowing that his office would be intact and available if he changed his mind. That way retirement wouldn't seem so definite, like such a huge change of life. If there was one thing he hated it was change. He'd always been a man who liked his routines, a predictable life. So why not keep his options open?

Back in his office, Fernando checked for messages and found none, so he put his feet up on his desk and started reading the *Independent*. He finished the first section quickly, scanning the headlines and hoping to find something he was interested in reading. When that failed, he tossed it in the trash and picked up the sports section. He was halfway through yesterday's professional baseball box scores when he heard footsteps on the gravel path leading to his office. He tossed the sports section in the trash with the other and took his feet off his desk. A paying customer, perhaps? He forgot all about retiring.

The footsteps stopped outside his door. He saw a very small shadow in the window. The shadow knocked lightly on the door.

"Come in," Fernando said.

The door opened and none other than Melissa Vigil stood in the doorway.

Fernando nearly fell out of his chair, diving down below his desk. He fumbled in his top drawer for his Smith & Wesson until he had it in his hand, just in case. Then he peeked over the top of the desk.

A cleaned-up Melissa Vigil, wearing khaki shorts and a new UNM T-shirt, stood in the doorway staring at him, hands on her hips and a look of surprise on her face. "What's wrong with you?" she asked. "I thought you were a private investigator?"

"Hey, you tried to shoot me, remember?" he responded.

When he saw she wasn't armed, Fernando got to his feet and placed his Smith & Wesson back in the drawer. They stared at each other across the small office for an awkward second.

Fernando spoke first. "So what's the occasion?"

Then Melissa smiled. "I just stopped by to apologize," she said, walking over and helping herself to the chair facing his desk. She crossed her legs and leaned back in the chair. Looked very relaxed.

Confused, Fernando wondered why the sea-change. Was she for real?

"Yeah, I wanted to apologize for my behavior earlier," Melissa continued. "I should have known you were only trying to help me. I'm real sorry for shooting at you. I just meant to scare you, but I realize now it was a crazy ass thing to do. See, I had a heart to heart talk with Sheriff Williams. She really helped me understand my situation and what Sven had done to me. I thought he was some sort of super hero fighting the system. What was I thinking?"

Fernando laughed. "A heart to heart with Jodie? I can imagine. I'll bet you did a lot of listening."

Melissa smiled. "Yeah, she gave me an earful. I guess I needed that, someone I trusted to give me advice. Like a mentor."

"Good to hear," Fernando said. "So what will you do now?"

Melissa pointed to her T-shirt. "I'm going back to school. I want to continue Sven's work."

Every muscle in Fernando's body tightened. He sighed.

Melissa noticed Fernando's reaction. "No, I don't mean the witchcraft and reviving dead people, all that crazy stuff. I'm going to get a certificate in Holistic Health and Healing Arts at the UNM Taos Branch. It's a thirty-hour program that I can do in a year, if I work hard. Let me show you."

While Fernando watched, Melissa took her cell phone out of a pocket in her shorts and booted up the Certificate in Holistic Health and Healing Arts screen. She handed him the phone.

Fernando saw classes in yoga and massage, even meditation, but of more interest to him were Introduction to Homeopathy and especially Introduction to Herbology. The Herbology course description read: "The class unveils the life-enhancing potential of herbs. Students will learn to identify herbs and to understand their properties and uses. They will also practice wildcrafting and making healing tinctures."

"Wow. Wildcrafting?" Fernando asked, because he couldn't think of anything else to say. He had no idea what that even meant.

"Gathering herbs in the wild," Melissa said. "Maybe that was what Sven was trying to do, but just got carried away. Went bat-shit crazy."

Fernando nodded. He felt like he was talking to one of his daughters, Flavia or Adela. He wanted to be positive, even though this herbology stuff sounded a bit like what Anders had attempted. So he kept his mouth shut.

Be supportive, he told himself. He'd learned that from raising his two daughters.

"Yeah, I'm on my way up to Taos to register for fall classes and find an apartment," Melissa said. 'My parents said they would pay my tuition and rent as long as I stay in school."

Fernando spoke finally. "Sounds like you're all set. I'm glad to hear it, Melissa, I really am."

"I just wanted to stop by and apologize," Melissa said. "Sheriff Williams said I should."

"No problem. I'm just glad to see you're safe."

Melissa stood up and smiled. Suddenly she reached over and threw her arms around Fernando, hugging him tight.

"Whoa—" Fernando said, hugging her back. Then he watched Melissa dance across the floor and out the door.

READERS GUIDE

1. Why does *Santa Fe Independent* reporter Fidel Rodriguez agree to meet an anonymous caller at the Cerrillos Hills State Park south of Santa Fe at eleven p.m.? What happens when he arrives?

2. When Rodriguez's wife asks Private Investigator Fernando Lopez to find her husband's killer, Lopez visits the Cerrillos Hills State Park and talks to the investigating officers from the Santa Fe County Sheriff's office. What does he find out about a previous murder of a woman discovered at the park visitor center that seems so bizarre?

3. Devil's Throne will become an important place and geographic marker in the story. What exactly is Devil's Throne?

4. Lopez learns from Santa Fe Police the identity of the dead woman found at the Cerrillos Hills State Park Visitor Center: Gloria Chavez. Why do they refer to her as "mummy woman"? What else do they know about her?

5. The next day Lopez learns that another mummy woman has been found at Cerrillos Hills State Park. When he arrives to investigate, what transpires?

6. Lopez and Santa Fe County Sheriff Jodie Williams follow the ambulance to Christus Saint Vincent Hospital in Santa Fe, where the second woman is taken. What does the woman, semi-conscious, say out loud that will be important in pursuing her assailant?

7. The second woman, April Lux, wakes up and tells Lopez and Williams more about her assailant. She tells them that he had a strange Nordic name and claimed to be an anthropology professor at the University of

New Mexico. Also, doctors at the hospital tell them about the results of April's blood work. Why are the doctors puzzled by the results of her blood test?

8. Meanwhile, Lopez learns that Essentia, the sex shop next to his office, will be working with Gabe Rivera, a *curandero* from Galisteo, to offer medicinal herbs for a variety of ailments and conditions. What is *Curanderismo*?

9. Lopez visits Gabe Rivera's shop in Galisteo and learns that his shop has been burglarized and some of his herbs stolen, including Wolfsbane. What is Wolfsbane?

10. April Lux remembers more about being kidnapped by her assailant and taken to a strange place near Devil's Throne. How does she describe the place? She also recounts what her assailant told her about his work as an anthropologist researching old witches' tales. Explain what he does with these witches' tales.

11. Lopez visits the Anthropology Department at the University of New Mexico in Albuquerque and interviews its chairperson, Doctor Hugh Satterfield. When Lopez relates what April Lux had said about her assailant, Satterfield recognizes the assailant as Sven Anders, a graduate student who was expelled from UNM. Why was he expelled? Satterfield also describes Anders companion, Melissa Vigil? What do we learn about Melissa Vigil?

12. Lopez finds the latest address on file at UNM for Sven Anders and visits the address in Albuquerque. Though the house is rented by someone else, Lopez finds Anders loading some of his belongings into a Toyota Tacoma pickup. What happens when they meet?

13. Lopez and Williams realize that Anders is finding his victims in the bars of downtown Santa Fe hotels, so they decide to set a trap for Anders using a female cop by the name of Laura Ortega carrying a GPS device as a pickup. On the second try Anders picks up Ortega and takes her to Devil's Throne in Cerrillos, where Anders attempts to rape Ortega. How does the encounter end?

14. Lopez returns to the area around Devil's Throne the next day by himself and finds Anders lab and living quarters. He also finds Melissa

Vigil. Describe the place. The next day Lopez brings Williams to the site. What happens?

15. Anders flees with Melissa Vigil. How and where are they finally located? In the confrontation that follows, Anders escapes but Melissa Vigil is captured. How does Lopez know where Anders is heading, thanks to Melissa Vigil?

16. The novel comes to a shocking conclusion at Gabe Rivera's herb shop in Galisteo. In the melee that occurs, Anders is shot and killed. Who shoots Anders?

17. What happens to Melissa Vigil? How does Lopez find out?

Printed in the USA
CPSIA information can be obtained
at www.ICGtesting.com
LVHW031112160424
777535LV00007B/475